# HUGO AND JOSEPHINE

Maria Gripe was born near Stockholm in Sweden in 1923. She has written many internationally successful and prize-winning books for children and has been awarded the Great Honour Diploma by the International Board on Books for Young People. The three books in this series were made into a film by Kjell Grade. Entitled *Hugo and Josephine,* the film won the first prize at the International Child Film Festival in Teheran in 1970.

*By the same author in Piccolo*
JOSEPHINE
HUGO

# HUGO AND JOSEPHINE

MARIA GRIPE

*With drawings by*
Harald Gripe

*Translated from the Swedish by*
Paul Britten Austin

## A Piccolo Book

PAN BOOKS LTD
LONDON

First published in Great Britain 1971 by Chatto & Windus Ltd
This edition published 1974 by Pan Books Ltd,
33 Tothill Street, London SW1

Originally published in Sweden under the title
*Hugo och Josefin* by Albert Bonniers Forlag, Stockholm

ISBN 0 330 23940 6

*Printed in Great Britain by
Richard Clay (The Chaucer Press), Ltd, Bungay, Suffolk*

# I

IT'S the first day of term. Mama and Josephine are on their way to school.

It's a lovely morning. Crickets are chirping in the grass, and the wind sighs.

Josephine has a bow in her hair and shiny new shoes on her feet. The wind is rather strong, so now and again Josephine has to make sure her bow is where it belongs.

The wind raises dust on the road, and she has to be careful not to let her shoes get dusty.

As they approach the school, other mothers with other children are coming from all directions. They all look rather ceremonious and solemn. Everyone is going the same way. To school.

Nearly all of them say 'good morning' to Mama. They recognize her because she's married to Papa-Father, who is the Vicar. Josephine curtsies, and the other mothers give their children a little shove to make them curtsy, or bow their heads to Mama, too. Everyone is very polite today.

Josephine has seen some of the children before, though she knows no one. Many of them have teased

her, called her old-fashioned: but today nothing of that sort is heard. All the children walk silently beside their mothers. The mothers talk to one another, but the children don't say a word. Even though they know each other and play in the village every day, they are all behaving like perfect strangers. They just stare at one another.

There's Edvin Pettersson, with his stalwart mother. Usually he is the terror of the villagers – but the pride of the village children. A little savage; no one is safe from him. A head of tousled hair, which makes itself seen everywhere. But today he just stands there. A bit shy. His hair combed down with water. Pale. Cowed. He throws angry glances at all the other little urchins in the gang, all as newly scrubbed as he himself. No one utters a sound.

Today is a very special, solemn day.

The tall school gates stand wide open. On the flagpole in the middle of the playground the flag is flying high. Everyone looks up at it. The school bell rings.

Josephine squeezes Mama's hand. Together they go in through the school door, up a stone staircase, the most worn-out staircase Josephine has ever seen. The walls echo. Inside, there is a peculiar smell, strange and awesome. A bit scared, Josephine holds her breath a moment; then, slowly, she breathes in the air. She sighs delightedly. So this is how a school smells! Now she knows.

It's quite another world they are entering, Josephine and all the others. Tomorrow she'll have to go into that world all on her own, without Mama. So must all the children. This thought strikes Josephine just now, and she squeezes Mama's hand hard.

Suddenly Mama stops.

'Here it is! Your classroom, Josephine.'

They are standing in front of a tall pale-blue double door. A group of mothers and children gather outside it. The blue doors are still closed. In the middle of all that blue, two shiny gold door handles gleam. On one of the doors a mysterious sign is shining, also gold. And under the sign is a square white piece of paper.

Mama says the sign is a three, meaning this is the third classroom in the corridor. And on the white bit of paper is written the name of their teacher: Ingrid Sund.

Oh – so that's teacher's name – Ingrid Sund – Ingrid Sund. Josephine tries the name out to herself, over and over. She finds it a very remarkable name.

She cannot take her eyes off the blue doors. Behind them is – the teacher. High up beside one of the doors a key hangs quivering on a hook. That must be the teacher's key. Of course, it must fit the keyhole beneath the golden door handle. As she stands there staring at the keyhole, from which little bunches of light dance into the corridor, Josephine feels little shivers of deep respect, excitement, and purest happiness passing through her.

Now a boy sticks out his head and tries to peer

through the keyhole. It's Edvin Pettersson. His plastered-down hair has begun to dry, and it's sticking up again. He's beginning to look like himself. But as he stands there, peering in, the door handle above his head is suddenly depressed downward. In the nick of time Edvin's mother grabs him by the arm.

'Edvin! Must I be ashamed of you?' she says, red in the face, dragging him away. But now no one is thinking about Edvin.

For the blue doors are flung wide open. Sunshine

streams out. And there stands the teacher. Ingrid Sund is standing there, smiling, right in the middle of the doorway, holding out her hand. She asks them all to come in.

But Josephine clutches her mother with both hands, hanging back. Tugging and pulling at Mama's coat, she whispers urgently:

'We've come to the wrong place, Mama. This isn't my classroom. She's not my teacher. My teacher doesn't look like that! She isn't fat, like this lady.'

But Mama takes a firm grip on Josephine's hand, telling her in a stern voice not to talk nonsense. Of course they haven't come to the wrong place! This is Josephine's classroom, and Ingrid Sund is her teacher. And that's enough.

Mama is not to be reasoned with. Without more ado, she pulls Josephine into the classroom.

Josephine looks anxiously about her. There's certainly nothing wrong with the classroom. It has big windows with yellow curtains and on the window sill are flowers. The desks and chairs are yellow, too. Yes, it's certainly her classroom. But the teacher ... Josephine won't look at her. The disappointment has been too great. It's more than she can bring herself to believe that behind those blue doors with the golden door handles was nothing but a perfectly ordinary young woman. Rather fat, too. She looks like someone's aunt. She can't possibly have such a beautiful, such a remarkable name as *Ingrid Sund*. Josephine gives a sigh of resignation.

She is shown to her desk. The others have already sat down in theirs. She sits in her row, but she has her desk to herself. Actually, there ought to be two children at each, but there are more desks than children. There's one place left over. What a pity, it's the one next to Josephine. It must be because no one knows her. Not yet! It'll all be different, later on.

Now Miss Sund is standing on the platform. On either side of her stand all the mothers, looking at their children.

Miss Sund talks to them. She makes a little speech, jokes and laughs. But Josephine is hardly listening. She is lost in thought. Staring straight ahead, she sizes up the little figure on the platform. Her doubts whether this can really be Ingrid Sund grow and grow.

It's not easy to keep a poker face in such extraordinary circumstances, but Josephine decides not to unmask the teacher just yet. First, she'll have a word with Mandy, at home in the kitchen. Mandy will know. Together, they'll find the real Ingrid Sund. Calmed by this thought, Josephine pays more attention to what the teacher is saying. Now, she's going to do the register. When she calls out their names, they are to stand up in their desks. It will be fun.

'Ruth Adolfsson,' says teacher; and at once a little

girl jumps up. Teacher looks at her and says she may sit down.

'Sven-Erik Alm!' A boy pops up at the back.

'Ann-Mari Andersson!' Another little girl leaps up, curtsies, and is told to sit down again.

'Hugo Andersson!'

Nothing happens.

'Hugo Andersson!' says the teacher again, a bit louder. Everyone looks around with curiosity. No one gets up. 'Isn't Hugo Andersson here?' asks the teacher. But there is no answer.

'Is there anyone in the class who knows Hugo Andersson?' she asks. They all just shake their heads.

'So, no one knows why he hasn't come to school?' she says. She goes on calling the others.

Like so many jack-in-the-boxes they pop up, one after another, out of their desks, slightly red in the face, under the stares of all the others.

'Anna Grå,' says the teacher, suddenly. And for Josephine everything stands still. You could hear a pin drop where she sits. Her heart flies up into her throat, but she can't move a muscle.

Anna Grå – that's the name Josephine used to have – ages and ages ago; she doesn't like it and doesn't want to be called by it. She'd almost forgotten it! Instead, she calls herself Josephine Joandersson. And everyone calls her Josephine. Everyone!

'Anna Grå!' The teacher's voice is heard again. But Josephine just sits, as if turned to stone. Now it is doubly clear to her: this *can't* be her real teacher. The real one would have known that Anna Grå no longer exists. She'd have called out Josephine.

'Isn't Anna Grå here, either?' the imposter asks; and then Mama goes up to her and says quietly, but so that everyone can hear:

'Yes, of course she is.' And looking at Josephine she says, a little more loudly: 'Get up now, Josephine, dear.'

Then Josephine obeys and meets teacher's eyes – pierces her with a look – while Mama explains that at home she is usually called Josephine. Josephine, she says, isn't used to being called Anna. That's why she didn't get up at once. The teacher laughs. All the mothers laugh. But not the children. They stare at her. All of them.

'Oh, so it's like that, is it?' says the teacher. 'But here in school we must all be known by our proper names. Mustn't we, Anna, dear?'

Josephine looks at her without replying. And when teacher says she can sit down, she goes on standing. Because it is Anna Grå the teacher is addressing, not her.

'Sit down, Josephine, dear,' Mama's voice is heard saying: and instantly Josephine sits down.

The roll call continues. But Josephine is no longer interested. Nothing is as she had imagined it. The seat beside her gapes emptily, the teacher isn't the right one, and . . .

On the way home they buy paper to line her desk, pretty blue paper with red stripes, and a pencil box with two pencils and an eraser. She gets a little notebook with kittens on it and a bookmark in the shape of an owl into the bargain.

She begins to feel better. But then, unexpectedly, Mama says:

'You'll have to try and get used to being called Anna Grå at school, Josephine dear. It can't be helped. And Anna's a lovely name.'

Then Josephine understands.

Anna Grå hasn't vanished, isn't forgotten. She has come back. She has been lurking stealthily somewhere in the background. It wasn't Josephine Joandersson who started school today, as she'd imagined. It was Anna Grå.

# 2

As if Josephine didn't know what a proper school-teacher looks like! She's known that for ages. Ever since she saw the picture in Mandy's women's magazine.

That must have been at least a year ago.

Every week a magazine arrives for Mandy, who cooks the food at the vicarage. Once there was a long story in it all about a schoolteacher. And Mandy read it and told Josephine everything that happened to this teacher. And that was quite a lot, believe me: everyone wanted to marry her, and all sorts of trouble and adventures followed. In the end she fell into a lake and got terribly wet and ill and nearly died. Then she married the doctor for safety's sake. Just as well, of course, in case she had any more trouble.

There were pictures of this schoolteacher in the magazine, too, one picture a week. Josephine feasted her eyes on her. She looked like a queen – beautiful, sorrowful, and stern.

After Josephine gets home from registering, she digs out a picture of the schoolteacher, which she has been keeping in the drawer of her bedside table. With a troubled expression on her face she ponders over it.

She isn't so childish as to imagine that she'll get exactly the *same* teacher as in the story. But she knows what a proper teacher ought to look like. Not like Ingrid Sund, anyway. Certainly not.

First of all, she shouldn't be plump. She shouldn't have fair hair. In the story it was clearly written: *Her hair gleamed like silk, black as night.*

Ingrid Sund's hair looks like a scrubbing brush. Her eyes are like two little shallow puddles. A proper teacher ought to have eyes like the ones in the magazine. Josephine will never forget the way they were described: *Her eyes were deep as wells, black and full of enigmas.* Wasn't it remarkable, when you come to think of it, that she was the only one who saw that there were no enigmas in Ingrid Sund's little round eyes?

That Mama should know anything about schoolteachers is more than one can expect, because she never even glances at women's magazines. Only Mandy does that. Josephine must talk to her about it. She takes the picture and runs down into the kitchen.

But grown-ups are really very odd. You can never be sure they'll understand. Mandy usually is one of the more reliable ones. One doesn't usually have to say

16

much before she grasps what you're driving at. But today it's as though her brain wasn't working properly.

She doesn't even remember the story in the magazine, though she herself read it and told it to Josephine, week after week.

'I can't remember all that rubbish,' she says now. 'Such a lot of silly stuff one reads. That's not worth remembering.'

'But Mandy, you said every word of it was true,' says Josephine, indignantly.

'Oh, did I really? But I didn't mean it, Josephine. I just read you what was in the magazine. Everyone knows that all that stuff is just make-believe.'

Mandy casts an uninterested glance at the picture Josephine shows her. She has forgotten that, too.

'Oh, I see. Yes, she's a beauty, all right, that school-teacher. But real people don't ever look like that. They've prettied her up, you see: she's not like ordinary people.'

Josephine gets angry with Mandy. She asks her straight out how she can read such silly lying magazines.

'Well, one has to have something to amuse oneself with,' says Mandy, a little nonplussed. 'Though it was stupid of me to tell it all to you, Josephine, so that you believed it. I never thought you'd take it so seriously.'

There is a moment's silence. Gloomily, Josephine contemplates the picture of the beautiful schoolteacher while Mandy searches for a pepper pot she's mislaid.

It's just as well, Josephine thinks, that schoolteachers don't necessarily look like the one in the picture, which Mandy says is just made up. Even so, Ingrid Sund isn't the right one – something inside Josephine tells her this. And she says so to Mandy.

'I've never heard such rubbish in all my life,' says Mandy, busying herself in the kitchen. 'Of course she's your proper teacher. You'll see. And don't you imagine anything else. As for all that stuff and nonsense in the magazines, don't pay attention to it; because it's only a lot of make-believe.'

Josephine finds the shaker, which has rolled under

the kitchen table. She picks it up and hands it to Mandy. Then, with extreme gravity, she says:

'Anyway, she isn't a *real* teacher. She doesn't even call me Josephine. She thinks my name is Anna Grå.'

Then Mandy shows even she is hardly to be trusted any longer.

'Well, isn't it?' she asks, and begins peppering her stew, as if peppering were the only important thing in the world.

# 3

NEXT morning, Josephine goes off to school alone. Mama and Mandy stand at the window and wave. The sky is grey. It is drizzling, the chill wet grasses swish around her knees, and puffs of damp wind rush out at her from side-roads. Brr, she shivers. How cold and wet and silent and lonely it is!

As soon as she comes within sight of the schoolhouse, she begins to run. The playground is already full of children. Everyone gets there early the first few days.

Josephine immediately recognizes a couple of girls in her class. They are standing together, and she approaches them. They look her up and down in silence. When a yard or so away, she comes to a halt, a little unsure of herself, but happy.

She smiles but not too much. You have to take things by stages; she knows that.

Nor do they smile back: as yet they don't know her.

Soon that'll all be different. Soon she'll know all the children. Soon she'll know how to play all their games. The village children ask a lot of you. There's so much they know, which Josephine doesn't. But now – at last – she will be one of them.

The girls stare at her without a shadow of a smile. Then they put their heads together in a close huddle. A

rustle of whispers reaches Josephine. First one, then another head half-turns in her direction. Someone looks at her sideways, with her hand to her mouth, whispering with the others.

Then one of the group says aloud:

'Only boys bring knapsacks.'

She doesn't say it to Josephine. She says it to the others. But of course Josephine hears it. And all the girls wave their satchels at her. They all have the same kind, little schoolbags with zip-fasteners and handles.

And there stands Josephine with her knapsack. It's true; it's a boy's knapsack, her big brother's, when he was small. But he hasn't used it much. It looks quite new.

She quickly slips her knapsack off her shoulders, so as to hold it in her hand. But that doesn't make things any better. The others still stare at her. But their eyes are full of indifference. She just doesn't interest them, and she realizes that. It's the fault of the knapsack. They turn their backs on her and go off.

At last, the school bell rings. Everyone rushes towards the door, jostling one another and trampling on each other's toes. A teacher is standing in the door, trying to get them into line.

Josephine begins to feel a bit more cheerful. In the scuffle she recognizes Edvin Pettersson. He has had his hair plastered down again today, but he is neither pale nor serious. Red in the face, he bites at an apple. His pockets bulge with apples. He shoves and nudges and yells at the top of his voice. After a moment he is beside

Josephine, proudly patting his bulging pockets. Laughing, he takes out an apple, looks it over, takes out another and suddenly – even though they don't know each other – hands her the bigger of the two.

Josephine is struck dumb. They have a whole orchard of apples at home, but she hasn't the gumption to eat up the apple. She stuffs it into her bag.

'Try one,' says Edvin, plunging his teeth into his. 'I've got lots of them.' Then he gives Josephine another. And one to a boy who's standing beside them. Then Josephine eats hers. It's the tastiest apple she has ever eaten.

Today, the teacher is waiting for them outside the blue door. She has the key in her hand, pointing with it as they line up in double file out in the hall. Josephine tries to stand beside Edvin but isn't allowed to. Instead, she finds he's standing just behind her. His pockets are still bulging, and the teacher asks him to take out the apples. He piles them up in a huge heap in the boot locker.

The teacher looks so amazed that Edvin finally offers her an apple. At first she says she doesn't want one, but then she changes her mind and stuffs her apple into her bag, to keep.

Then she opens the doors. They go in.

There they sit, staring at each other, Miss Sund and the children. Outside, the rain drizzles down: but the flowers are gay in the windows and the curtains are yellow.

The teacher opens a great big book. In her hand she holds a pencil.

'Now, I must make sure I really know all your names,' she says, and begins the roll call.

Josephine turns pale. That horrible name – is it going to plague her today, too? Is every day going to begin like this?

This time they don't have to get up when the teacher calls out their names, unless she doesn't recognize them.

'Hugo Andersson,' she calls. But he isn't at school today, either.

'I can't understand this,' says Miss Sund. 'Is there really no one here who knows anything about Hugo Andersson?'

No, no one has so much as heard of him.

'I'll have to look into this,' says Miss Sund, and goes on to the next name. Name after name – most of which she does not remember.

Then it is Josephine's turn. Stiff as a post, she sits there, filled with dread. The teacher lifts her eyes from the attendance book. Josephine waits. The teacher looks at her – a long while. Josephine looks back. In her eyes there is a little gleam of defiance; in the teacher's eyes, laughter. The teacher blinks. But not Josephine.

Much against her will, Josephine finds she doesn't

dislike Miss Sund's eyes quite so much as she thought she did, allowing for the fact that she isn't the right teacher.

'And you, my dear,' says Miss Sund, slowly, after a moment. 'I recognize you all right.'

She hasn't said her name! Miss Sund quite simply skips over it and goes on to the next one.

Suddenly Josephine's heart is so light, it is like a balloon inside her. She could float up to the ceiling.

After that, everything is all right.

They line their desks with paper. And Josephine has the same pencil box as most of the others, a wooden one, with flowers on the lid.

Then Miss Sund hands out reading books to them all. They are allowed to turn the pages, look at the pictures, and they must promise to make paper covers for the books when they get home. The letters are easy to learn.

*Thy Bright Sun*, too, is easy to sing. Miss Sund plays on the harmonium and sings it first. Then they sing it.

School is easy. Easy as anything, thinks Josephine as she goes home. As easy as easy! None of the others live in her direction, and the rain is pouring down. She is alone and wet as a drenched cat. But happy. She sings *Thy Bright Sun* so loud it can be heard a mile off. And inside her knapsack the new reading book jiggles up and down with Edvin Pettersson's apple.

# 4

JOSEPHINE is thoughtful.

What a lot of things she has to learn at school! She's been going for several days now and can read a lot of words. But she has done most of her learning during break and after school is over. That's when you learn the really important things — things of which she'd never dreamed.

Miss Sund's little lessons in the pretty reading book are easy and don't take much thought: but her school-mates' lessons are hard. They fill poor Josephine's head from morning to night.

Fancy ever thinking she had only to start school to get to know all the children in the village! It's by no means so simple as that! She thought she'd learn all their games in no time and be allowed to play with them. But days have gone by, and they still don't let her join in at all.

The strange thing is, they all know who she is without even asking. Even some who are not in her class. But she hasn't the remotest idea who they are. She knows nothing about their mothers and fathers, but they know everything about hers.

'Your dad's a clergyman, isn't he?' they ask, in the most innocent way.

'Yes,' Josephine answers.

'*We know,*' they say then, and look at Josephine strangely. She can't understand why. It sounds as if they knew something she doesn't.

'D'you know what a hop-pole is, eh?' someone asks. But Josephine doesn't answer, because she's not sure.

'It's a clergyman, see, who believes he can get to heaven just because he's so tall,' says a big girl. And then all the others laugh till they scream.

'Tell the old blackbeetle to stay down on earth,' she yells after Josephine. The fact is, Papa-Father is tremendously tall. That is why she can't bring herself to call him Father, as he once wanted her to. His head, which is so far above hers anyway, would then be even higher above her. She has to say Papa-Father, so as to reach up to him.

'Ask the old boy if it isn't a bit draughty about the ears up there,' says the big girl on another day. Her name is Gunnel. Although she's in the second class, she's nearly ten, for she had to stay back one whole year.

Everyone wants to be friends with Gunnel because her father owns the sweet shop in the village street. He lets her take as many sweets as she likes. But Josephine can never be Gunnel's friend, she realizes, because Gunnel says she 'despises' Josephine. Josephine isn't too sure what 'to despise' means; but she's sure it's something not everyone can do. One has to be a bit better than others. Like Gunnel.

'I *despise* you,' says Gunnel, looking at Josephine out of narrowed eyes.

The words make Josephine tremble. Gunnel looks cold and superior when she utters them – and so handsome, too! It's horrid, being despised by her.

If the others say they despise her, too, they do it to copy Gunnel. But Josephine feels that somehow only Gunnel is really good at it. Only she can despise in such a way that Josephine's blood runs cold.

Sometimes Gunnel brings whole bags of sweets to school. Then she stands on the school steps like a queen, visible from all over the playground. No one else is allowed to stand up there. If someone does, he gets a kick and is in Gunnel's bad books for a long time.

There she stands, alone, handing out a sweet. She reaches into the paper bag and looks searchingly out over the mob of eager faces below her. They wave and shout.

'Me! Me!'

'You know me! You and I've always . . .'

At last Gunnel makes up her mind – calls to some fortunate one to come forward. Sometimes she changes her mind just as he reaches her and gives the sweet to someone else instead. And the poor disappointed wretch has to trudge off ashamed and empty-handed.

Sometimes Gunnel holds up a bar of chocolate, waves

it round in the air, juggles with it, and suddenly throws it down into the crowd.

'Catch as catch can!' she shouts; and all the children fling themselves on the tasty morsel, falling on top of one another in heaps, fighting and yelling. Gunnel stands on the steps, cheering them on and scolding them.

One day Josephine is standing in the crowd – not because she'll get anything, but because it's exciting to watch. That day Gunnel has brought a particularly big bag with her. Many children have already had some of its contents, but there's still a lot left.

Now Gunnel holds up a whole packet of toffee. She looks from one to the other. Then her eyes come to rest on Josephine, and a gleam comes into them.

'The Vicar's kid, there! In the brown coat! Come here a moment, Josephine, or whatever you're called!'

A shock goes through Josephine. Gunnel means *her*! Is *she* to get the packet of toffee? In her amazement she stands rooted to the spot. Amazed and embarrassed. And scared too.

'Hurry up, silly!' cries Gunnel.

Josephine's ears grow pink with excitement. Has Gunnel turned nice, all of a sudden? Has she stopped despising Josephine?

A boy in Gunnel's class shakes his head at Josephine.

'Don't go,' he says. 'She's just teasing you.'

Gunnel rattles her packet of toffee. The temptation

is too strong for Josephine. She pushes her way through the crowd, up to the steps. Stands at the bottom step.

'Come on up, then,' says Gunnel. 'Don't you dare?'

There's a dangerous glitter in her eyes, and as she goes up the steps Josephine feels horribly exposed. Her knees quake.

Upright, queenly, Gunnel stands there, one hand on her side, waiting. She's nearly twice as tall as Josephine.

From the crowd below comes whistling, mocking

laughter, and insults. Gunnel stretches out her arm and points at Josephine.

'Fall down on your knees, and ask really nicely!' she commands.

Josephine stands rooted to the spot. As if she hadn't understood.

'Well?'

Gunnel holds the packet of toffee under her nose.

'Do you want it, or don't you?'

Josephine just stands there ... There's a breathless silence. Everyone waits, tense, to see what's going to happen.

'Hasn't your father even taught you how to pray? What sort of a nutty clergyman is he, then?'

The laughter grows. Gunnel becomes bolder. She goes right up to Josephine, shoves the whole bag under her nose.

'See how full it is? It's all yours if you kneel down and beg for it. Say: "Nice, kind Gunnel, give me a few sweeties, even though I'm such a dirty little Stone-age brat." Go on, say it!'

Then Josephine wakes up. She practically falls down the steps again, into the mob, which hoots with laughter. She is hot with shame.

'Pooh, pooh, pooh!' Gunnel spits at her, from above. 'I despise you, despise you. And you can tell your nutty clergyman-father he can teach his own kids how to pray, before he gets up and babbles in church.'

The last thing Josephine sees before she manages to push her way out of the crowd of children is Gunnel, dancing wildly about and scattering the contents of the packet of toffee and everything else from the paper bag all over the delighted children.

'Catch!' she yells in ecstasy. 'Go on, jump for it!'

That evening Josephine sits quietly at home. Behind her reading book, she looks from one member of the family to another. How could she know they were such a lot of failures? Papa-Father sits under the yellow glow of his reading lamp, a big thick book on his knee, his hair a little white and tousled, smiling slightly; he is far away in another world.

So he's a nutty clergyman, is he? A hop-pole?

Mama over there in the window nook, her little, bouncy, soft bob of hair at the neck, sorting out a hopeless muddle of yarn, staring sleepily, a little helplessly, at the tablecloth that must be ready for the bazaar, but never is . . .

So she's a she-monkey, is she, a self-important old so-and-so?

Josephine catches a glimpse of her own face in the mirror on the wall, but doesn't want to look at it. It's no fun looking at a dirty little brat. Especially one who dates back to the Stone Age, whenever that was.

# 5

ONE morning Josephine finds she isn't walking to school all by herself, as she usually does, because no one lives on her side of the village.

Who can that be, walking ahead of her? It's a boy, and he must be going to school, because he's got a knapsack on his back.

She hurries to catch up with him. Since he is ambling along, it isn't difficult. He walks a little bent, hearing and seeing nothing. He's busy with something. What could it be?

Now Josephine is right behind him, but he doesn't hear her. He's absorbed in whatever it is he's doing. She sees a sunburned neck and a striped shirt that's a bit on the big side and carelessly stuffed into black shorts that are too long for him. A pair of braces, green as grass, hold them up. No other boys wear braces, only old men.

Josephine wonders if she should overtake him or . . .

At that moment he stops but doesn't turn round, doesn't look in her direction. She stops, too, and looks to see what he is doing. In one hand he has a piece of wood, in the other a knife, carving away so that the chips fly.

'Hello,' says Josephine, after a while.

He doesn't look up, but answers,

'Hello there!'

'What are you doing?' she asks.

'Carving,' he says.

'Is it going to be a boat?'

'No.'

'What, then?'

'A troll.'

'Can I see?'

'When it's ready you can.'

And she has to be satisfied with that. They stand silently a while – he carving, she watching. He still hasn't looked up at her.

'Shouldn't we go on now? Aren't you coming to school?' Josephine asks, after a while.

'There'll be time for that, too,' he replies calmly.

Josephine hasn't got a watch, she may be wrong about the time; perhaps she left early this morning.

'Do you live in this direction?' she asks.

He doesn't reply at once, just examines his bit of wood and takes a couple of digs at it with his knife. Finally his answer comes:

'Sort of . . . Maybe . . .'

'I've never seen you before.'

'No.'

'I'm in class one. Where are you?'

'In the same one, I suppose.'

Josephine looks at him, reflecting. His arms and legs are thin, his neck too. He's a lot thinner than she. He's not at all like the others. How is it she hasn't noticed him before?

'But you aren't in my class,' she says.

'Aren't I?'

He's only interested in his bit of wood. If he's the same at school, it's not surprising that he doesn't know who's in his class.

'What's your teacher's name?' Josephine continues her cross-examination.

'Can't remember.'

'Ours is Ingrid Sund.'

'Oh?'

The conversation dies away. It's no fun just asking questions. Or only answering them, if it comes to that.

'We may be late,' says Josephine, at last. 'Hadn't we better hurry?'

'I've got to finish this little troll first,' he replies, and his knife goes so fast it flashes in the sun. He's in no hurry. He just sits calmly among the flowers by the roadside.

Josephine doesn't dare wait any longer, and he doesn't seem to care what she does.

'I'll go on, now,' she says, a bit hurt.

' 'Bye,' he replies, still not looking up. He hasn't, not even once. Josephine has never met a stranger boy.

Of course, she's late getting to school, but that doesn't matter so much. Others are late, too, and Miss Sund is quite used to it. She doesn't get very cross, just says they must soon learn to keep better time.

But hardly anyone ever arrives as late as Josephine does today. She barely has time to sit down at her desk before the bell rings for the next class.

The others have been given little arithmetic books with pictures of tiny red apples and oranges and suns and gingerbread biscuits shaped like old men. And here and there a few figures. Josephine is worried that she won't get her sum-book, just because she has come so late. But at the next lesson she gets it.

Counting is easy. Writing numbers, too. Josephine draws numbers that lean towards each other and sway about like trees in a storm, says Miss Sund.

In the breaks they exchange bookmarks. Unfortunately Josephine hasn't any with her, though at home she has a whole boxful of little angels. She's had them for ages. They're very pretty, but all their heads once came off, and she had to glue them on again. Some of the angels have swapped heads, but that, in Josephine's opinion, has only improved their looks.

Sometimes, when she looks at herself in the mirror, she thinks it's a pity people can't change heads, too. She could do with a change. In school are lots of girls she'd be only too happy to swap with. Gunnel, for example. Gunnel is pretty. Josephine doesn't like her. Because she's silly. And nasty. And conceited. And scornful.

Even so, there's no one she'd sooner be friends with. That's strange, she thinks to herself. And she's ashamed of it. To want to be friends with her tormentor . . ..

After school today Josephine makes a new acquaintance. She is standing a little way off, watching the others exchange bookmarks. Suddenly a girl comes running up to her and gives her one. A shiny red bouquet of roses, which is only a little bent at the bottom.

'You can have this, because I'm sorry for you,' says the girl, seriously.

'No,' says Josephine, embarrassed, but joyfully accepting the bookmark.

'Yes, I'm sorry for you,' says the girl obstinately. 'My mother is, too. Maybe you can have one more,' says the girl, fishing out a little hare, which has only lost the tip of one of his ears. Red in the face, Josephine protests:

'You don't have to be sorry for me, I've got lots of bookmarks with angels on them at home.' The girl looks at her through incredulous blue eyes.

'You can be somebody to be sorry for, even so,' she says wisely, but adds, thoughtfully, 'How many angels have you got?'

'Well, heaps,' says Josephine. 'So many you can't count them.'

The girl's eyes become even rounder than usual. They're always rather round, anyway, like all the rest of her.

'Really?' she says. 'Have they got curly hair?'
Josephine nods.
'And wings? And float on clouds?'
'Oh, yes.'
The girl sighs and looks at Josephine reflectively.

'Angels make the best bookmarks, don't you think?'
Yes, Josephine must admit she thinks so. She proudly remembers her box at home.

'I haven't got one single angel,' says the girl sadly. 'No one wants to swap their angels, because everyone's collecting them. And they've run out of them at the shop.'

Josephine feels all warm with pleasure.

'You can have some of mine,' she says. 'I'll bring them tomorrow.'

'Promise you won't forget?' asks the girl in her serious way.

'Yes,' replies Josephine. 'I promise.'

They exchange serious and solemn looks as they part outside the school gate.

# 6

NEXT morning Josephine is in a hurry to get to school. She has the box of bookmarks with her, and half runs. It's a lovely day, hot, with blazing sunshine. Almost like summer, even though it's September. Butterflies are fluttering across the road, and in the woods birds are still singing. But Josephine has neither eyes nor ears for them; she just runs and runs. After all, isn't that girl waiting for her angels?

Suddenly, from the ditch, a voice:

'Hello there!'

Josephine stops short, looks around. At the edge of the road a head is sticking up, half hidden by grass and flowers. The boy again! There he sits, calm as can be.

'You never came to school yesterday,' Josephine reproaches him.

'I didn't get there in time. They shut that school so early; it's crazy.'

Josephine comes closer. What a strange boy. She must

explain to him that school goes on for several hours. The simple fact is, he's lazy. But then he says, by way of explanation:

'It's because of the troll. You see, I couldn't get him finished.'

'Where is it?' Josephine wonders, climbing down into the ditch. 'Can I see him?'

The boy looks up calmly.

'Nothing came of him. In the end I didn't have enough wood left to work on; so I had to begin all over again.'

He looks so convincing that she realizes at once why the troll has to come before school. No question about it. Now he has a new piece of wood in his hand and has just begun to carve a ball. She mustn't disturb him. He has to concentrate, and she has to get to school in time to give the girl her angels before it starts.

So she clambers out of the ditch again and says good-bye to the brown nape of his neck.

'Do you think you'll have time to get there before we finish today?' she asks, cautiously.

'I should think so. There's going to be time enough for school.' He consoles her.

And Josephine leaves him and runs on. She thinks he's odd – but not incomprehensible, as Gunnel is. If it hadn't been for the angels, she would have stayed a while.


The girl is waiting at the school gate, where they parted yesterday. Josephine can see her from afar. There she stands, still as a statue, one arm hooked round her satchel, the other resting on the gate. Just as she did yesterday. Just as if she'd been standing there all night, waiting. At last Josephine arrives.

She's hot and out of breath; her hair has been flying all over the place and hangs down in her eyes.

'Have you been running?' asks the girl, as she stands

there so serious and tidy, with her hair in short thick little braids.

Josephine nods.

'Have you brought the angels?'

Josephine gets the box out and lifts the lid. Suddenly she's afraid they won't do because their heads once came off, but she needn't have worried.

'Oh, they're so pretty,' sighs the girl, with a little lisp. 'And the fair-haired ones are almost prettier than the others.'

'You can take whichever you like,' says Josephine, who in her joy is almost ready to give the girl the whole boxful.

But she's not that kind of girl. She is honesty and justice itself, as she stands there, choosing from among the angels. She wants only three, she declares. One flying, one sitting, and one standing, all as blonde and chubby as herself. In exchange, Josephine can choose from among *her* bookmarks.

Mostly, she has flowers and chubby little girls with skipping ropes and garlands of roses. Josephine decides on a white dove surrounded by forget-me-nots and holding a white letter in his beak.

'You've got good taste,' the girl says, appreciatively. Then she takes out a pencil, folds the letter in the dove's beak, and writes: 'MEMRY OF KA.'

'There's no room to put all of Karin, but it doesn't matter. It can be shortened,' she says, and in this way Josephine gets to know that her name is Karin. Then she hands Josephine the pencil and one of the angels she has chosen.

'You can write on the back. It's just as good.'

Josephine is happy, but a bit confused. She doesn't know whether she can write 'MEMRY OF' as well as Karin did, because she's never written it before. But she tries, does her best anyway, and it's not too crooked. And 'JOSEPHINE' looks all the better. She has been

46

able to write that for a long time. Karin gets the book-mark, but looks at it in astonishment.

'Josephine?' She asks. 'Isn't your name Anna? Anna Grå?'

Josephine turns bright red.

'No,' she says, in a tone of voice that brooks no con-tradiction. Karin looks dubious.

'Isn't the Vicar your daddy?'

'Yes,' says Josephine, 'But that doesn't stop my being called Josephine.'

'Sure,' says Karin. 'I just thought someone said your name was Anna, though of course you can have several names. Like me.'

Then Josephine learns that Karin has three names. She is called Karin Erika Magdalena Westerlund, and is the policeman's daughter.

'A policeman is sort of the same as a clergyman,' Karin explains. 'My daddy tries to stop people from behaving badly and sinning, too.'

Josephine's self-confidence grows when she hears that Papa-Father and Karin's daddy have so much in com-mon. Karin says:

'Sometimes my daddy has to put people in prison when they've done some horrible sins. Does yours?'

Josephine isn't quite sure about this, but doesn't want Papa-Father to be any less powerful than Karin's daddy.

'I think so,' she replies evasively, but Karin opens her

eyes very wide and looks sharply at Josephine.

'I don't think he does,' she corrects her firmly, shaking her head.

Right is right. The church belongs to Josephine's father, but the prison is Karin's father's. And Josephine secretly has to admit to herself that Papa-Father would sooner see people sitting in church than in prison.

But it's hard to get people to come to church nowadays, she knows, and says so to Karin.

'Not like prison,' says Karin, proudly. 'My daddy says it's overcrowded at times.' Josephine feels a bit squashed.

Then Karin tells about her mother, who works at the post office, can write and count on a machine. She's a telephone operator, too, and knows how you put through telephone calls. And sometimes when there's thunder and lightning, the lightning strikes just where she is sitting. It's terribly dangerous. Once she turned blue in the face from lightning – as if she'd been eating blueberries.

Karin's mother belongs to dozens of clubs and societies, and her father is in both a teetotallers' association and a choral society.

Josephine is impressed. Feverishly, she searches about in her mind for something remarkable to tell Karin about her own parents. Unfortunately there isn't much she can boast about. Not compared with Karin's!

Though of course Papa-Father can use a typewriter — and she says so. And when Karin asks how many fingers he uses, Josephine at once sees a chance of showing off.

'One, of course,' she says, importantly. 'Just this one.' For she fancies it must be a lot harder to write with only one finger than with all of them at the same time. Unfortunately, it isn't, as Karin tells her. *Her* mother writes with *all* her fingers! Otherwise you can't write properly. Josephine feels squashed again, but Karin is kind and consoles her.

'One finger is better than none,' she says.

'Sometimes he pokes with his thumbs, too, I've seen,' says Josephine, encouraged.

'Good,' says Karin, and taking Josephine protectively by the arm, she draws her over to the schoolhouse, for now the bell is ringing. On the stairs they have to part. Karin isn't in the same class as Josephine. She's in the first form, too, but another part of it.

At break they meet again, and now Karin tells Josephine about the house she lives in. It is a big square house, next to the post office. Pale green, with a red roof. And lots of roses in the garden. Hasn't Josephine seen it?

There is furniture in the garden with an orange parasol, she tells Josephine. And a bird bath with a little stone mermaid. Really, hasn't Josephine seen it?

Josephine is ashamed of being so slow-witted as not

49

to have noticed this wonderful house, though she's been down to the village often. But Karin isn't offended. Just astonished. And she promises to invite Josephine home. They'll drink lemonade under the parasol and sit there and look down on the traffic going by. As if they were sitting in a real café, she promises. Josephine is overwhelmed.

What bothers her is that there isn't much she can offer Karin in return. They've only got their old vicarage, but that's hundreds of years old. No parasols and no mermaids, either.

'It doesn't matter,' says Karin, understandingly. 'Anyway, it's more fun asking someone home than being invited out yourself.'

Josephine is dumbfounded. These words she recognizes immediately. She's heard them in church. Out of Papa-Father's own mouth! Well, not exactly, but much the same: 'It is more blessed to give than to receive.' Josephine looks at Karin with deep affection. And admiration. Karin must be terribly wise. Josephine isn't. She never utters any words of wisdom. Sometimes she can think them, but she never gets them out. Something's always in the way.

She gives a little sigh, and smiles unsurely at Karin.

'You ought to be a clergyman,' she says, 'you talk so wisely.'

Karin gives her a serious look.

'I'm going to be a hairdresser,' she says. And then Josephine is terribly afraid she's said something silly, but as usual, Karin overlooks it. She starts painting a vivid picture of the feast they'll have when Josephine visits her.

Overcome with gratitude, Josephine takes out her biggest bookmark – the one with three angels floating among flowers on a woolly cloud. To show she is not wholly unworthy of being allowed to indulge in the lemonade feast under the orange parasol and look at the artificial stone mermaid, she gives it to Karin.

# 7

It's the last hour of the day. The teacher is just teaching them a song about a chicken. Sitting at the harmonium, she plays and sings in a loud voice:

> There was a chicky-bird, whose name
> was Prettyfluff,
> And she went out to take a walk . . .

Then, suddenly, the door opens. She stops playing. Everyone looks at the door. There stands a familiar figure – familiar to Josephine although not to the others. Amazed, they stare at him. It's the boy from along the road.

The teacher gets up.

'Good afternoon to you,' she says. 'I haven't seen you before. What do you want?'

The boy strides into the room. He isn't the least bit shy.

'It's time to begin school.'

'Oh? But you don't belong in here, do you? Tell me the name of your teacher. Then we can find her for you,' says the teacher, smiling.

'Well, you see, I don't know. I went into the class-room next door, too, and that teacher said I was to come in here.' He jerks his thumb towards the next class-room. In the class you could hear a pin drop. The teacher looks a little nonplussed.

'Haven't you ever been to school before?'

'No.'

'Wasn't your mother here at the roll call, either?'

He throws her a reproachful look.

'What's the sense in bringing your mother to school?' He looks out over the class, as if wondering what the others thought about it. He has unusually blue and expectant eyes. Josephine sees, too, that he is thin in the face and rather pale. Only the nape of his neck is brown. Which is not surprising, since only his neck gets any sunshine. His head is always bent over his little pieces of wood.

Now the teacher looks even more nonplussed. She says, weakly:

'I don't suppose you are Hugo Andersson?'

'Yes, that's just who I am,' replies the boy, self-confidently. And as he hears his name, his face lights up.

53

Then the teacher goes over and shuts the door behind him. As if trying to gather her thoughts, she moves hesitantly, looking at Hugo with amused astonishment.

'So, you are Hugo Andersson,' she says slowly. 'In that case, you do belong in here. We'd been wondering where you'd got to.'

'Oh, have you?'

'Yes,' says the teacher, 'You see, you are a bit late.'

Hugo's clenched hand brushes the matter aside.

'I'd have come before,' he says, nonchalantly, 'but I didn't have the time, Miss. This school shuts so awfully early. How could I have known that? I've been on my way several times, but I never got here before the doors were shut.'

Miss Sund says she thinks it's a good thing Hugo got here eventually, anyway. She is beginning to recover from her astonishment, and hopes Hugo will find his way from now on.

'Find my way? I can always do that. It's getting here on time that's harder,' Hugo explains.

Now the teacher begins looking around the class to find a desk for Hugo. Only one is free. It's the one beside Josephine, who, of course, is terribly excited. Is she going to have someone to sit next to?

'Shall I put you there?' says Miss Sund, as if to herself. She looks thoughtful.

But Hugo goes over with firm steps to Josephine.

'Hello,' he says, and holds out his hand. Josephine takes it.

'This'll suit me fine,' he says, and sits down beside her.

'Yes, I suppose it will have to,' says Miss Sund.

But Hugo gets up again.

'I'd best say hello to all the others, too,' he says, and begins to go around the class, from desk to desk. He shakes hands with them all. A scraping sound comes from the desks.

All the children are very solemn and polite. Hugo asks them their names, and, politely, they tell him.

'Same Johansson as down at the mill?' he asks one of the boys.

'Perhaps it would be better if you made each other's acquaintance afterwards,' says the teacher, faintly. 'It takes up such a lot of time ...'

'Can't be helped, have to be polite, you know,' Hugo corrects her. 'Particularly when one hasn't been here from the start. Is your aunt the one who lives by Karrvik Creek? No?' he goes on, making conversation.

'You're the spitting image of an old woman who lives up at Norrasa. Is that your granny? No? Oh, well, can't be helped.'

Everywhere he sees likenesses and relationships, but nothing ever fits. Miss Sund tries to interrupt him. It's impossible.

By the time he has gone his rounds and flops down at his desk, next to Josephine, the teacher has become quite jittery.

'Now we really must make haste,' she says. 'Hugo must have his books and ...'

Hugo looks at her protectively.

'No hurry, Miss,' he says. 'Take it easy. You're as red as a fire engine.'

This remark makes the teacher no calmer.

'Aren't you going to take your knapsack off, Hugo, and hang it on the back of your chair, like all the others?' she asks, a little shrilly.

'Maybe I ought to,' says Hugo, and obediently starts to slip off his bulging knapsack. Then there's a loud crash. The top wasn't properly closed, and a shower of birch bark, wood, pebbles, and moss flies all over the room. Everything that can be picked up in the country-side comes tumbling out onto the floor.

The silence in the class is breathless, but all around Hugo there are crashes and thuds.

Hugo dives down among his possessions. Josephine helps him collect them. Edvin Pettersson rushes to their aid. Two other boys, too. All the others get up, but the teacher stops them.

'No more help is needed now,' she shouts.

Hugo is most meticulous about getting back all the things he has lost. Again and again his calm voice is heard:

'Somewhere I had a bit of juniper wood. You can tell it by its smell. There it is! Take a sniff, boys. Smells nice, doesn't it?'

The piece of juniper goes the rounds; everyone must have a sniff of it.

'Perhaps we should get on with our work now,' says the teacher, helplessly.

From between two of the desks Hugo's head pops up and informs her that there isn't too much missing.

'There're just a few acorns and a little bit of heart-wood. The kind that makes such nice little pipes, you know.'

At last he has all his treasures collected in a heap on his desk. He sorts them out, making a last check to be sure that nothing is missing, before stuffing them all back into his knapsack. Relieved, Miss Sund watches them all disappear.

'I must say,' she observes, 'I always thought a knap-sack was for schoolbooks.'

'There's room for them, too,' observes Hugo.

Now teacher brings out Hugo's books. She exhorts him to take care of them and make paper covers.

Interested, Hugo examines everything. He looks at the pictures and pronounces an opinion on them:

'Must be fine to be able to draw like that. Only thing is, it all becomes so flat, when it's just drawn. Not like when you carve, that's something you can take hold of.'

Several times the teacher opens her mouth. Then shuts it again. She looks like a fish out of water. In the end, she has to interrupt Hugo to make herself heard at all. She realizes that Hugo doesn't understand, she says, but in school children have to sit still and be quiet. The teacher does the talking, and the children just answer when the teacher asks them a question.

Hugo listens attentively to this, but looks frankly astonished.

'Now that's odd,' he says.

'What's so odd about it?' the teacher asks.

'There's no sense in our answering, when we don't know anything. We're the ones who ought to ask the questions.'

Then teacher explains the matter over again, explaining that Hugo will certainly understand it all much better when he has made a start on his lessons.

She brushes her hair out of her eyes and sits down at the harmonium. Now, she suggests, they'll sing again. She begins to play. Immediately Hugo makes his voice heard, praising her playing.

'Not bad,' he says appreciatively. 'But an accordion's a lot snappier. Can you play the accordion, Miss? My father, he's wonderful at it, and I can, too.'

Teacher says she can't, and Hugo generously offers to bring his accordion and play for her. But teacher says that in school they have to stick to the harmonium.

'Well, that'll do, too,' Hugo consoles her, and then listens in silence. After a while he searches in his pockets and brings out a little object and puts it in front of Josephine.

'It's that troll I told you about,' he whispers. 'You can have it.'

# 8

THE following days are eventful. But difficult, too, particularly for the teacher. Hugo and Josephine are late for school every morning. They're never in time for the first lesson.

Teacher scolds them, and Josephine looks guilty. Really, she doesn't want to get there so late, but what can she do? Hugo pays no attention to what teacher says. He doesn't think it's all that important.

'It's not so easy to find time for everything,' he replies calmly, when the teacher scolds him.

Now Josephine and Hugo come to school together every day. And though they meet much earlier than before, it's almost impossible to find time for all the things Hugo has to attend to along the way, and then to get to school on time.

Hugo regularly begins his day by hunting for what he calls 'wood for trolls and things'. And Josephine helps him do it. It's the least she can do, she thinks, after being given one of his trolls. 'Trolly,' she calls it, and it is one of her most precious possessions.

It's great fun, strolling about the countryside with Hugo. He sniffs about like an animal and recognizes every type of tree, every flower. If he can't tell what it is by looking, he uses his sense of smell. He sniffs at everything.

'You wouldn't get far without a sense of smell,' he says.

When Hugo has gathered the wood he needs for the day and returned to the road, he begins carving; to walk along idly doing nothing is impossible for him. There is no way to make him hurry, and Josephine doesn't want to run ahead on her own.

It's a real problem.

The teacher is not sympathetic. As each day goes by her face becomes sterner when she sees them.

One morning, when as usual Hugo and Josephine come drifting down the corridor about an hour late, they hear singing coming from the classroom.

'Are they singing about that silly Prettyfluff again?' says Hugo sarcastically. 'It's just stupid to sing about chickens like that. Let's wait until they're finished.'

But Josephine has an idea. While they sing, all the children stand in a circle round the harmonium, with their backs to the door. And the teacher, who is sitting

in the middle, can't see out over the classroom. Supposing she and Hugo just slip in silently and take their place in the circle? Miss Sund might think they'd been there all along. Hugo approves of the idea.

Soundlessly, they open the door. The children are bawling away about the chicken. No one is looking towards the door, as it closes after Hugo and Josephine. They manage to slip into their places in the ring, without anyone noticing them. Quickly, they begin singing away innocently.

Perhaps all would have gone well, if only Hugo could have put away his bit of wood. But he goes on working at it as he stands there. He is carving a whistle.

Suddenly, in the middle of the song, a piercing note is heard. Instantly, the teacher stops playing. There is a painful silence.

'WHO WAS THAT?' asks Miss Sund, looking around with stern eyes.

'It was me,' Hugo answers. 'I was just trying to see if I could get those high-pitched notes on my little whistle.'

Teacher gets up. She looks far from pleased. Her glance goes from Hugo to Josephine.

'Oh, so you're here, now,' she says. 'This cannot go on. My patience is at an end.' She tells the children to sit down – all except Hugo and Josephine. She takes them out into the corridor. She looks like a thunder cloud and says they might just as well stay away altogether as come so late.

'If it happens again, you can go home,' she says. 'You just must understand that school has to come before everything else now.'

Josephine says nothing. She is ashamed. Hugo is serious, but doesn't find it so easy to hold his tongue. With a worried air he looks at the teacher, and says:

'There're such a lot of things that have to come before everything else, it's not easy.'

Then the teacher's stern eyes become softer. She, too, looks more worried than anything else.

'So I see,' she says, 'But it's just not good enough, Hugo dear. It simply won't do.' She looks from Hugo to Josephine. 'Couldn't you help Hugo to come on time? Instead of arriving late yourself?'

Before Josephine can answer, Hugo does.

'She's done what she could, but I'm not so easy to handle.'

'You must take school seriously, Hugo,' says the teacher, and tries to conceal a little smile with a cough. 'You *must*.'

But then suddenly Hugo looks aggrieved. Standing there, legs wide apart, he sticks his thumbs in his grass-green braces and says:

'I do! I take everything seriously. I always have.'

'I don't doubt that, Hugo,' says the teacher with unexpected softness. 'But in that case you can certainly get here on time, too.'

Hugo scratches his head, a little embarrassed, perhaps a little nonplussed, too. He looks up. A light comes into his unusually blue eyes.

'I agree with you about that, Miss,' he says. 'I will!' Then, pulling his right fist out of the depths of his pocket, he stretches it out to her. Solemnly, they shake hands.

Karin is a bit jealous of Hugo. What she would like most would be to have Josephine all to herself. Yes, even though Josephine is always with her at break. Hugo stays with the boys. He is teaching them to carve, and they cluster eagerly around him – not only boys from his class, but from the whole school, even ones who are much bigger.

Karin thinks Josephine talks too much about Hugo. A sulky little look appears around her mouth whenever Hugo is mentioned. And she always sees to it that they stand as far away from him as possible.

She doesn't say anything nasty about Hugo. She isn't like that. She just wonders what it is that is so remarkable about him. She can't see it, she says.

But everyone else can.

When Josephine and Hugo go home from school together, many long looks follow them. Most of the children would like to live in her direction now. Since Hugo came to school, she has been treated with a certain respect. No one teases her in his company.

Even Gunnel behaves herself. It's true that her eyes still shine scornfully whenever she meets Josephine, but that's all.

Gunnel's star is beginning to wane. In spite of the

bags of candy. Sometimes she even has to stand there by herself with them. The fact is, Hugo isn't remotely interested in sweets.

'Sticky Stuff!' he says with loathing, and offers them sorrel and pine gum from the woods; everyone thinks they taste much nicer.

These are happy days; Josephine is no longer an outsider. She has Karin. And Hugo. Some of his radiance falls on Josephine.

# 9

Now the great day has come – the day when Josephine is to have her lemonade party under the orange parasol.

Wednesday, October 10th is a great day in Karin's family. It's Karin's seventh birthday, and her father, whose name is Hjalmar, celebrates his 'name day' – because that's the day's name in the Swedish calendar.

Karin has been talking about this day for several weeks.

Josephine knows exactly what Karin's father is going to get. A tie and hair lotion from Karin's mother. Socks from Karin's granny. A matchbox with sea shells on it from Karin's aunt. And a toothbrush from Karin herself.

Josephine was with her when she chose the toothbrush. They had it with a red, a blue or a green handle, so it wasn't easy to choose. In the end they agreed on a green for the sake of variety, since the tie from Karin's mother was blue and the socks from her granny red.

As for herself, Karin has guessed that she's going to get a jumper with a cap to go with it, which her granny has knitted. From her aunt she'll probably get crayons, because that's what her aunt usually gives her. From her mother Karin has asked for dolls' clothes and a wash-tub.

'Maybe there'll be some dolls, too, because they go with the clothes, don't you think?' Karin asks Josephine.

'Yes,' Josephine thinks so, too.

'But you're not to give me anything,' says Karin suddenly.

This makes Josephine embarrassed. She assures her that of course she will.

'No, because everything's so dreadfully expensive, so you mustn't,' says Karin. 'The only thing I've seen that's cheap is a doll's hairbrush with comb and mirror they've got down at the store. Together they cost one kronor, seventy-five öre. But you really mustn't buy them.'

Josephine goes bright red in the face, and doesn't know where to look. The fact is, she has already gone and bought just those things, since Karin was talking about them yesterday. That's why she is so terribly embarrassed as Karin goes on:

'They have pink ones with pale-blue butterflies on

the back. They're terribly pretty, but you mustn't get them for me. You can get them in blue, too, with red butterflies, but I think the pink ones are prettiest. Which do you think are prettiest – pink or blue?'

Josephine wriggles unhappily under Karin's searching gaze. It isn't easy to keep a secret.

'I don't know,' she replies evasively. Karin gives up and begins talking about what they'll eat and drink under the parasol. And what they're going to do at her house. Everything has been planned down to the last detail, because Karin likes to have order in all things. She wants to have everything arranged far in advance. What she's going to get, what they'll eat, and what they'll do. She'd even like to know in advance what they're going to say to each other. That would be best of all, though of course it's impossible.

Now the day has come.

After school Josephine goes up to Karin. She has red shoes on her feet and a bow in her hair. Her present is done up in a pretty parcel, tied with a red silk ribbon.

It's a wonderful Indian summer day, though one can feel autumn in the air. The ferns have turned red. Yellow leaves come fluttering down. Already a few trees are almost bare. But the sun is shining, and the air is mild.

Karin stands waiting at the gate of the green house.

She has her best things on. A satin dress and – *nylon stockings*. Her chubby little legs gleam like a couple of shiny salmon in the sunshine.

'I've been given them by my aunt,' Karin says, lifting one leg up for inspection. 'Real nylon!'

Josephine stands there stricken dumb with admiration. Then she remembers her own present, and hands it to Karin.

'Many happy returns.'

'But I said you weren't to give me anything,' says

Karin excitedly, tearing open the parcel. As she takes out her present she looks satisfied.

'Oh, Josephine, thanks! How *could* you guess it was *just* what I wanted?' she says, pretending surprise and doing it rather well. She looks at herself in the little mirror, and smiles.

'They had it in blue, too,' says Josephine. 'I was so worried you'd sooner have had that.'

'Oh no,' says Karin, still putting it on. 'Pink is my favourite colour. You've really got very good taste.'

'Do you think so?' flutes Josephine.

'Yes, just the same as me,' Karin lisps back.

Karin's garden is smothered in red roses and a blaze of autumn blooms. It's not a very big garden, and it slopes down towards the road. In front of the house is a terrace. There stands all the garden furniture with the gigantic orange sun parasol. The feast has already been laid out on the table. Karin's mother did it before going off to work at the post office. The table groans under all the delicious treats.

'We've *bought* the bread,' Karin says, her face shining with pride. 'The birthday cake comes from the New Cakeshop in town and we've got all sorts of fizzy drinks instead of fruit juice. It tastes much nicer, don't you think?'

Yes, that's what Josephine thinks, too. Her mouth is

watering. But before they begin their banquet, Karin says they must see the whole house.

Solemnly and ceremoniously Josephine walks at Karin's side through the green-painted house Karin has talked so much about. She can see her own reflection in the freshly polished floors and in the shiny furniture. Here everything is new and fine, not old and worn-out as it is at home in the vicarage. But there's more room to move about at home, for there's more space between the chairs and tables. Here everything is crammed very close together.

Josephine admires Karin's birthday table with the dolls' clothes and the washtub and the jumper and knitted cap.

She is also allowed to look at her daddy's name-day table. There lie the socks and hair lotion, the tie, the matchbox, and the toothbrush from Karin.

To see all these things in reality almost seems a bit of a come-down – she's heard so much about them! They ought to be giving off some mysterious secret radiance, but they don't. In spite of everything, they look just like ordinary ties and socks and toothbrushes. Josephine looks shyly at Karin, who stands with her head cocked a little to one side, smiling to herself. Karin seems to know how to extract a secret radiance from these things anyway.

'What a good thing we took the one with the green handle!' she says.

'Yes,' says Josephine.

Then they each take a doll from Karin's room and go out into the garden. Josephine has been allowed to borrow a big doll with a sailor jacket and cap. It is nearly as big as she is, and once belonged to Karin's mother.

'You must see the bird bath,' says Karin. They go over to it.

In the middle of the bird bath sits a little mermaid with a fish's tail and curly hair on her head.

'It's made of artificial stone,' says Karin, stroking it. 'Isn't it lovely?'

Then Josephine gets a crazy idea. She takes the jacket and cap off the doll, steps into the bird-bath and puts them on the mermaid.

Karin, terrified, opens her eyes wide.

'You're crazy!' she says. But then throws her arms around Josephine and bursts out into uncontrollable giggles. Then she takes the scarf off her own doll and puts it around the mermaid's neck. In a huge fit of giggles they tie a checked ribbon in a bow around the fish tail.

Then they sit down together under the parasol, in a wonderful humour.

Karin pulls the caps off the bottles so that they pop, and without spilling a drop on the cross-stitched table-cloth, pours out the lemonade. Then she serves sponge-cake and biscuits. Finally the creamy birthday cake, with meringue.

The sun shines down through the parasol, casting a warm yellow glow over the table and everything on it. And on Karin and Josephine too. In this unreal light, Karin's little round face shines as if transfigured.

Josephine looks at her – enchanted. And Karin looks at Josephine; they smile happily at each other.

Now and again they look down the road beneath them. It's like sitting in paradise, Josephine thinks, floating above the village.

Down there it's an ordinary weekday. An old man cycles past, a woman hurries off with her clinking milk bottles, some children gape and stare . . .

Suddenly Josephine seizes Karin's arm.

'Do you see who's coming?' she whispers. 'Gunnel.' Carrying shopping baskets! She's been shopping and looks sulky and tired. Their triumph is complete. If only she could see them. If only . . .

They begin to sing at the top of their voices. She can't help hearing *that*!

Yes, and she does. Now she's looking in their direction.

They hold each other's hands, tra-la-la-ing for all they're worth, as if they hadn't a care in the world, pretending not to see Gunnel. But as she comes closer, Karin shouts in an unnaturally loud voice to Josephine:

'WOULD YOU LIKE SOME MORE BIRTHDAY CAKE?'

'YES, PLEASE!' yells Josephine.

'YOU CAN HAVE AS MUCH AS YOU LIKE!'

Gunnel comes to a momentary halt and pulls a

horrible face at them. But they pretend not to see her. Afterwards they almost die of giggles. After Gunnel has disappeared they lie doubled up on the grass.

Now the bus comes and stops, right at the bottom of the garden. An old man and a couple of old women get off and toddle away. The driver gets out a moment and lights a cigarette. He leans against a tree, looking at them curiously as he smokes.

From their golden world they smile down at him, waving graciously. He waves back.

When the bus leaves again, Karin whispers blissfully to Josephine:

'Well, isn't this just like sitting in a real café?'

# *10*

It is reading time in school. There they all sit, with their reading books open before them on their desks. They have a whole page to read. Some are having trouble. They are not as attentive as they should be.

Out in the corridor there is a tremendous commotion. Although the doors are closed, every sound forces its way in. Out there some of the bigger children are fighting and quarrelling and giggling. Obviously, no one can read in such an uproar.

'Ssh-ssh-ssh! Be quiet. You *must* be *quiet*! We're doing our lessons in here, and you're disturbing us, ssh-ssh-ssh,' the teacher says, clapping her hands.

For a while quietness reigns. But then the noise begins all over again. First cautiously, then worse and worse. She gets up . . .

But then Hugo stands up, too.

'Sit down, Miss, let me deal with them,' he says

obligingly. And the teacher, somewhat taken aback and uncertain about what to do, remains standing at her desk.

The noise outside reaches its climax. Stalking over to the door, Hugo throws it wide open, and legs apart, thumbs into his braces, stands there contemplating the uproar.

'SHUT YOUR TRAPS, YOU BRATS!'

Instantly, silence reigns. Placidly he shuts the door and goes back to his desk. Not another squeak is heard from the corridor. The teacher looks astounded. They go on with their reading. It is Edvin Pettersson's turn.

'JOE GOES FISHING. HE CAT ...' '*Catches*,' the teacher corrects him. Edvin goes on:

'THEN JOE TRIES THE FISH ...'

'*Fries*,' the teacher corrects him. 'Berit please go on.'

Berit does her work thoroughly. She reads the whole passage fluently.

'THE FISH IS BIG. MOTHER FRIES JOE'S FISH. THEN JOE EATS THE FISH. MOTHER KNOWS HOW TO FRY FISH, SAYS JOE. JOE HAS A BROTHER. HIS NAME IS JOHN. JOHN IS BIG. JOHN WANTS SOME FISH, SAYS JOE. NO, SAYS JOHN.'

'Good,' says the teacher, and Berit looks around proudly.

Then a boy who always has a runny nose starts reading. He snivels and stammers and hisses through his nose, so it all sounds terrible, and soon teacher lets him off.

'Hugo can go on,' she says. But not a sound is heard from Hugo. He just sits there scratching his neck.

'What's the matter, Hugo?' asks Miss Sund. 'Have you lost your place in the book?'

'No.'

The teacher makes a sign to Josephine.

'Show him where we are,' she says, but the silence is just as deep. 'Well, Hugo, go on, read!' says teacher, a trifle impatiently.

'Those last words in the last sentence, what were they?'

'You can see for yourself, Hugo.'

'No, I can't.'

'Begin with "Mother fries," ' whispers Josephine.

'Now I know,' says Hugo, and rushes through the whole piece at top speed. The teacher looks suspicious.

'That went rather quickly,' she says. 'Read it over again. Begin at the beginning.'

Hugo babbles through it from beginning to end. He reverses a couple of sentences and mixes up Joe with John, but otherwise it's correct. But the teacher doesn't look at all pleased.

'Now listen, Hugo, my little fellow, tell me, how are you reading, really?'

'I read it by heart, right through,' Hugo replies, his eyes shining.

'H'm, did you?' says the teacher. 'But now we'll take it *bit by bit,* and *slowly*. Let me hear now.'

'But I can't. That isn't something I've learned.'

'How extraordinary!' says the teacher. 'How can you learn your lesson by heart without learning it bit by bit, Hugo?'

'I listened to the others, of course.'

'In other words, Hugo, you haven't done your homework.'

'No, I haven't; there was so much I had to do yesterday. I didn't have time, see?'

The teacher passes her hand through her hair and looks at Hugo helplessly.

'My dear Hugo,' she groans. 'Whatever shall we do? How can I teach you to read, when you won't do your homework?'

'Don't you bother your poor head over teaching me to read, Miss,' he says consolingly. 'That's something one has to teach oneself. There'll be time for that, too ...'

They look at each other a moment, Hugo and the teacher. Hugo is a lean little fellow, but he looks strong and protective. The teacher is big and strong, but just now she looks as if she were badly in need of assistance.

'Hugo,' she appeals to him. 'I'm here in order to teach you to read, am I not? Haven't you understood that?'

Hugo makes a deprecating gesture. He looks more terrified than anything else.

'No,' he says. 'There's no sense in it. What, just to teach us to read what's in books?'

'It's *fun*,' says teacher, 'but it makes me unhappy when you don't bother to do your homework.'

'Oh, I wouldn't be worried about that, if I were you – no, really I wouldn't,' says Hugo, with warmth and conviction.

The teacher looks at him seriously.

'Oh, I do. I do worry about it, Hugo,' she says.

All this happened on a Saturday. On Monday morning Hugo comes to school beaming with joy.

'Now I can read my book,' he says to the teacher. She looks a bit dubious. But it is as Hugo says. Suddenly he knows how to read. Not only the old lessons. He can read the entire book. The teacher is utterly perplexed.

'How on earth have you done that?' she wonders.

Hugo himself is filled with wonder.

'It was a bit tricky to begin with,' he explains. 'But then I opened my eyes like this,' he says, opening his unusually blue eyes. 'And then I stared hard at those little letters. The same way I search in the woods for little bits of wood to make things out of. And then I saw how they crept together, those little letters, just like little creatures on the ground. It all happened by itself. It wasn't so hard, just a bit tricky.'

# *II*

ONE day Hugo isn't waiting down by the road. He isn't at school either. He must be ill, Josephine thinks to herself. What a pity! But it often happens that the children miss a couple of days because of a cold. Particularly at this time of year.

Now it's autumn. Cold and grey. It rains often. And the wind blows. The mornings get darker and darker.

You have to wear raincoats and boots. Last time Hugo was at school he had a big black rain cape on, which stuck straight out from him so that he looked like a great flapping bird. That day it rained terribly hard. He must have caught cold. Such a long way he has to walk to school, too! They say he lives a terribly long way off, up in the woods.

The days go by. Hugo doesn't come. He must have been really ill. One day teacher asks if anyone knows how he is. But no one knows anything; he hasn't a telephone and no one knows how to find the way to his house. They don't know very much about him at all, for he hasn't been living long in this part of the country.

School isn't the same without Hugo. A listlessness comes over the class. It's sleepy and absent-minded during lessons. Nothing exciting ever happens any more.

To make things a bit more exciting, they begin squabbling. That is Edvin Pettersson's doing. Now, with Hugo away, he is the centre of attraction. He's fun, Edvin, and up to all sorts of tricks. But in quite a different way from Hugo.

Of course Edvin tried to make a racket and played tricks when Hugo was there, too. But he never really got going, perhaps because Hugo wasn't the least bit noisy. One might think so, but he wasn't. Hugo was bold and fearless in every inch of his being; he could answer the teacher back in the most astounding way. But a troublemaker – no ...

Sometimes when there was a lot of noise in the class, Hugo's voice made itself heard:

'Listen, you blockheads, you've got to be quieter. There's no chance to think with such a racket, and everyone carrying on.'

Then, usually, there was silence. No one was annoyed. Least of all Edvin Pettersson.

They all miss Hugo, but no one misses him as much as Josephine.

When Hugo came to school, all Josephine's troubles vanished overnight. Now they begin to pop up again. One after another.

Her classmates treat her differently.

Slowly but surely Gunnel regains her power over them. And she is worse than ever. She's always causing trouble now. She brings bags of sweets with her every day. She seems in a hurry to tease Josephine, for she knows that as soon as Hugo comes back her ravages will be at an end.

The odd thing is, Gunnel never tried her tricks out on Hugo. They have never exchanged a word. She kept out of his way. Something seemed to tell her he was stronger than she. Even though he was so much smaller.

But things aren't easy for Josephine now. Gunnel plagues her and torments her in every possible way. With unswerving accuracy she puts her finger on Josephine's weakest spots. Gunnel is a genius at tormenting others.

Now they have found out the secret about Josephine's name. No one had bothered about that before. Mostly they had just called her Josephine.

Of course, the teacher had sometimes said Anna – mostly when reproving her. Otherwise, she usually just nodded or pointed at her. But she never said Josephine, and this was something Josephine had got used to. Nor did it matter to her, as long as Hugo was in the class. She hardly thought about it.

But now things are different. The teacher says Anna more often – perhaps because Josephine is less attentive nowadays. At least the teacher says she is. She usually wakes her up by shouting 'Anna Grå.' That never fails. Instantly Josephine is wide awake.

Now her secret has leaked out and reached Gunnel.

'Your name isn't really Josephine,' she says scornfully.

'Yes, it is,' says Josephine.

'No, it isn't, because your name is Anna. ANNA! ANNA!'

And they all shout Anna after her. Wherever she goes.

'I despise you, Anna,' says Gunnel, her eyes narrowing, so that Josephine's blood runs cold.

One day Josephine is given a new hat. With high expectations, off she goes in it to school. She thinks it's exactly like all the other girls'. But it isn't. Only nearly. Not quite! It turns out to lack something most important. The girls look critically at her.

'There should be a brim in front. Yours hasn't got one. You look silly,' they say.

She is also given a new jumper, which is as similar to

the others as it could possibly be. So she thinks. But when she gets to school, all she hears is:

'It shouldn't be so high at the neck. It looks silly.' Her jumper is only *nearly* like all the others'. Like everything else about Josephine.

She begins to suspect the fault is in herself.

When one thinks of Hugo . . .

How can he be allowed to wear bright green braces – such as only old men wear?

How can he wear shorts that are too long for him? No one else does. All the other boys have long trousers. How can he come to school in a rain cape as wide as a tent? After all, the others have rain coats.

Why doesn't anyone tease him? Why doesn't anyone ever tell him he looks silly or stupid? It's odd, isn't it?

No – it isn't as odd as it seems. For this is the way of it:

Either you must be exactly like all the others. Or you must be completely different from them – as Hugo is.

You mustn't ever be *nearly* like everyone else. As Josephine is.

Something tells Josephine this is how it is. Even though she can't understand it.

# *12*

It is break. Karin and Josephine are skipping in one corner of the playground. Josephine can skip well now. Both backwards and forwards.

They are so busy counting their skips, they don't talk very much. Absent-mindedly they stare out into the air in front of them, skipping and counting.

Karin is the first to tire. She stops and stands looking at Josephine.

Suddenly she says:

'Hugo'll never come back to school. You'll see!'

Josephine stops instantly. Her heart skips a beat. Terrified, she stares at Karin. What did she say? Karin repeats it.

'Hugo's never coming back to school any more. You'll see!'

Terrible thoughts fly through Josephine's head. Is Hugo ill? Perhaps already ... She dare not follow the thought to its conclusion. She'd like to ask Karin, but can't get a word out. Karin is looking at her in the strangest way. Now she says again:

'He's not coming. And it's just as well.'

Josephine gasps. Everything goes black before her eyes. She has noticed that Karin is jealous of Hugo. But she never would have believed that Karin could say such nasty things. Josephine grips Karin by the arm and shakes her.

'How can you say such a thing! Are you crazy?'

Karin looks at her uncomprehendingly.

'Let me go,' she says. 'Can I help it? Is it my fault he isn't coming back, eh?'

'No,' says Josephine, 'but you said it was just as well.'

'It was my mother who said so. "Best as it is," she said.'

Josephine doesn't let go of Karin.

'Tell me what's the matter with Hugo.'

But Karin purses her lips and a scornful look comes into her eyes.

'Is he very, very ill?' whispers Josephine, beside herself.

'Who said he's ill?' Karin answers.

'But he isn't at school.'

'That doesn't mean he's ill, does it?'

'Has he gone away?' gasps Josephine.

Karin just shakes her head.

'Well, then, what's the matter?'

She looks at Josephine, and says in an important voice:

'I'm not allowed to say.'

Josephine suddenly lets go of her, staring at her as if she'd had her face smacked. *Not allowed to say!* There stands Karin, and knows something about Hugo which Josephine doesn't. And won't tell her!

'Why aren't you allowed to tell?'

Karin doesn't reply. She begins skipping again.

'Who said you couldn't?'

She skips so that her skipping rope whines. Rhythmically with both feet. Her lips tightly pursed, she stares stiffly into the distance.

The bell rings. And Karin goes off like an arrow across the playground, without waiting for Josephine. Without even giving her another look.

'You must tell me!' shrieks Josephine.

'Never!' screams Karin.

'You've made it all up! You're lying, and that's why you won't tell,' says Josephine triumphantly.

'I'm not allowed to, I tell you,' hisses Karin.

They stare at each other. Their eyes flash.

'I don't believe a word of it.'

Karin stops a moment to think. She feels insulted, not to be believed. She says, in a dignified voice:

'My father's a policeman, I'll have you know. It's he who has forbidden me to say anything.'

This should put an end to the matter. But not for Josephine.

'I'll bet he didn't,' she says. 'He doesn't know anything about Hugo.'

Karin draws a deep breath.

'Yes, he does, whether you believe it or not. And, so does my mother, because she's a telephone operator here, and she knows everything that happens here in the village, almost. But I'm not allowed to tell anything. So there!'

Josephine realizes she isn't going to get any further with Karin. There's nothing more she can say. Only:

'You're silly, silly, silly!'

And then runs off.

After that Karin stays with a girl from her own class at break. She doesn't even look at Josephine. It's as if they didn't even know one another. As if they'd never been friends.

It's terrible. It can't be true.

She has not only lost Hugo. She has lost Karin, too.

# *13*

MAY-LISE is the name of the prettiest girl in Josephine's class. Berit is the tidiest. They're always together. They share secrets that no one else is allowed to know.

One morning Josephine comes to school too early. They are to begin an hour later today, but Josephine forgot and left home at the usual time. Not until she reaches the playground does she remember.

When the bell rings for the other classes to go in, she stays outside. But it's cold and windy, so after a while she goes in.

No one is in the corridor. All the children's clothes are hanging there. From the classrooms comes a muted sound of singing and lessons being heard. The door to her classroom is shut, but the key is hanging on its hook. That means teacher is sitting inside. Quite right – there hangs her coat. And her big bag is on the galoshes locker.

Josephine goes out to the stairs and stands looking out of the window. But the schoolyard is deserted – there's nothing for her to look at. So she goes back into the corridor and sits down on a corner of the galoshes locker. She snuggles up behind a couple of coats. Rather long coats, which belong to the big girls.

Then she takes out her reading book and looks in it, waiting for the hour to pass. It's terrible how slowly time creeps by.

But after a while she hears footsteps and sees Ulla, who belongs to her class, come in swinging her satchel. Ulla is a thin, insignificant little girl, whom no one can quite understand. Like Josephine, she has no one to be with, but she doesn't seem to care. It seems she wants to be on her own. It's true, she goes with the others during break, but isn't one of them, even so. She never joins in. Just hangs around.

She's not much fun, but still Josephine is pleased to see her coming. Now they can wait together. She brightens up and calls out to Ulla.

'Did you forget we had the hour off, too?' she asks.

Ulla has already taken off her hat and begun to unbutton her coat when she catches sight of Josephine. Now she checks herself, and buttons it up again.

'No,' she answers, curtly. 'I always come on time.'

She doesn't seem at all happy that Josephine is sitting there. She puts on her hat again and goes. She's as unsociable as that. Josephine looks disappointed.

After a while footsteps are heard on the stairs again. And titterings. It's Berit and May-Lise, that's something you could tell a mile off.

But now Josephine doesn't bother to try and find company. She knows it's hopeless. Berit and May-Lise don't want anyone else. Particularly not Josephine. They are among the girls who usually play up to Gunnel.

Now they're standing there, tittering. They haven't noticed Josephine and she doesn't bother about them. She buries herself in her reading book.

She can hear them tiptoeing about and whispering.

What is it they're tittering about so helplessly now?

When she looks up, she sees them bent over teacher's big bag. They have opened it and are busy ransacking it. May-Lise is holding up a photo, and whispers, tittering:

'How crazy he looks. Do you think it's Miss Sund's fiancé?'

'Hee-hee-hee-hee doesn't he look silly?'

Josephine is astounded. She drops her book.

They give a jump and stare at her in terror. May-Lise pushes the photo back into the bag. And Berit tries to fasten the clasp. She fumbles with it and tips the bag over so that all its contents come tumbling out. There lies the mirror, cracked straight across.

'What are you doing here?' hisses Berit furiously at Josephine.

'What are *you* doing?' says Josephine.

Berit chucks all the contents of the bag back any old way. She can't fasten the clasp, so it has to remain half open on the galoshes locker.

Now all three of them stare at each other. Ashamed, not knowing what to do.

'Surely you don't think we were going to pinch anything?' says May-Lise weakly.

No. That thought really hadn't occurred to Josephine. But now, when May-Lise says it, she gets scared and doesn't answer.

'What're you running about here spying on us for?' says Berit, who is tougher than May-Lise.

Lamely, Josephine explains that she had forgotten they had the first hour off.

'We were only going to have a look at teacher's fiancé,' squeaks May-Lise. 'We weren't going to take anything.'

Josephine believes her. But she thinks it's nasty, even so.

'Are you going to run and tell tales?' says May-Lise, on the point of tears.

Josephine shakes her head. But Berit gives her a hostile look.

'If you do, I'll give you what-for,' she says. 'Come along, May-Lise.'

And off they rush.

Josephine just stands there and goes red all over.

Then the door opens. There stands the teacher. Josephine gives a little start, and the teacher looks at her in astonishment.

'Are you here already?' she asks. 'Have you forgotten you've got the first hour off today?'

Josephine nods.

'What a shame,' says Miss Sund in a friendly way. She looks around. 'I wonder if I put my bag out here or if I left it in the teachers' common room.'

Josephine turns pale. Stiff with horror, she stares at the half-open bag.

'But there it is, how careless of me,' says the teacher,

and suddenly wrinkles her brow. 'It's *open*!'

She takes up the bag and looks into it. She takes out the cracked mirror. Josephine stands rooted to the floor.

The teacher shuts the clasp with a little snap and goes towards the classroom, saying nothing. But just before she shuts the door she looks at Josephine again.

'Have you been here in the corridor long?' she asks.

'Yes – no – yes,' stammers Josephine.

'Has anyone else been here?'

Josephine doesn't answer. She shakes her head but doesn't dare look at the teacher. Miss Sund closes the door.

During the lesson she gives no sign. She hears their lesson and they have singing.

But just before the bell goes, she says unexpectedly:

'There's one thing I must ask you. Remember – never have any valuables or money in your pockets or leave your satchels in the corridor. I was careless about that today, and someone, I see, has been in my bag. My mirror is broken. So please remember that.'

Josephine feels all the blood rush from her head. There's a flickering in front of her eyes, and she doesn't dare turn around. She is aware of May-Lise's bowed head on her left. Berit is sitting behind her. Silence falls on the class. But a hand flies up.

'Ulla,' says the teacher, 'what do you want?'

A monotonous voice says:

'When I got to school, Josephine was already sitting in the corridor, all by herself.'

Everyone looks at Josephine.

'Ulla! What do you mean?' says teacher.

Ulla doesn't answer.

'What she means is that Josephine has been inside your bag,' says a boy, who thinks the whole thing is terribly exciting.

'Do you mean that, Ulla?' says teacher, astonished. But Ulla does not reply. 'Well?' says teacher.

'Noo . . .' is heard from Ulla.

'Then I can't understand what you mean,' says the teacher, impatiently. 'But I want you to know that I'm not so stupid as to think Anna has been in my bag. She may have seen who it was, I don't know, but . . .'

The teacher breaks off and looks at Josephine – or Anna, as she insists on calling her. Her nose pale, Josephine drops her eyes.

'You needn't say anything, my child,' says the teacher calmly. 'If there's anyone in the class who has done it, he or she will certainly tell me himself, or herself.'

The teacher doesn't say another word. The children wipe the blackboard. Then the bell rings.

Josephine leaves the room as quickly as she can.

If only she had Karin now. Or Hugo. But Karin

plays only with a girl in her own class. And Hugo has vanished.

During break she stands by herself in one corner of the playground, listlessly turning over her bookmarks.

Suddenly, someone puts an arm through hers in the friendliest way. It's May-Lise. There she stands, looking sweet and pretty and smiling at Josephine.

'You aren't angry with me any more, are you?' she says. 'It was all just in fun.'

No, Josephine isn't angry with May-Lise. She's just confused and feeling strange. She wants to answer May-Lise, but it's difficult. She can't get it out, what she wants to say.

May-Lise cocks her head and looks innocently at Josephine.

'It was Berit who wanted to do it,' she says. 'I didn't.'

She lays her arm around Josephine's shoulders and together they walk slowly across the playground.

'Berit thinks you're going to tell tales to the teacher,' she says.

Josephine shakes her head.

'Aren't you?'

'I'd never do that,' says Josephine.

'Promise? For sure?'

'Yes.'

Silent, they go on their way. When the bell rings,

Josephine sees Ulla and Berit together. They look strange. Inscrutable.

'Don't you think Berit's silly?' says May-Lise. 'We aren't friends any more.'

'Oh?' says Josephine.

'Ulla's silly, too.'

During the next lesson May-Lise smiles at Josephine whenever she looks in her direction. Josephine feels happier. May-Lise, the prettiest girl in the class, with her dark curly hair – just imagine, supposing they could be friends!

And at break May-Lise comes over again. There go Ulla and Berit together, looking as silly as can be. Well, let them, thinks May-Lise.

'And then we'll be rid of them,' she says loud enough for Berit to hear.

When Karin sees Josephine and May-Lise together she looks utterly amazed. She could never have imagined that! She follows them with her gaze and her friend has to pull her pigtail to capture her attention.

Gunnel comes over and gapes at May-Lise:

'Oh, so you've fallen as low as that, have you? That Anna thing! I'd never have believed it of you!'

May-Lise looks terribly crushed.

Throughout break, a whole little drama is going on.

Josephine walks solemnly arm in arm with May-Lise.

Maybe they haven't so very much to say to each other. But they're together, and that's the main thing. Just now, at least.

At the end of break, May-Lise suddenly says to Josephine:

'Know what? I know something!'

'Do you? What?'

'It's a terribly secret secret, of course.'

'Is it?' Josephine says, while May-Lise shows off a bit.

'The sort of thing one tells one's best friend.'

Josephine's heart starts thumping. Expectant, she looks at May-Lise. This is something she'd never have dreamt of! That they'd even be best friends!

'I'm not *allowed* to tell, see? Do you promise not to tell anyone?'

Of course Josephine promises. She's feeling almost giddy with excitement. And with the wonderful sense of belonging, which comes with a secret.

'Do you swear?'

'Yes.'

'On the Bible? Remember your father's a clergyman, and he can send you to burn in hell if you don't keep your promises.'

Josephine promises; not that she thinks Papa-Father would let her burn in hell. But she swears the biggest oath she can think of.

'Good,' says May-Lise, and looks around her. Ulla and Berit are over there in the background. Karin and that girl from her class, too. So much the better.

May-Lise cups her little hand around her pretty mouth, opens her eyes wide and whispers in Josephine's ear:

'It's about Hugo Andersson.' She makes a pause.

Josephine presses her ear against May-Lise's hand.

'His daddy's in prison.'

# 14

JOSEPHINE sits at home, stunned. In front of her lies Trolly, which Hugo gave her. She looks at the doll sorrowfully. It is a little lumpy knotted troll, with two grey stones for eyes and moss on its head. It looks as if it had just crept out from the root of some ancient tree.

*Hugo's daddy in prison!*

Only thieves and other bad people go there. Hugo's daddy can't have . . .

Her thoughts go round and round. So that's what Karin knew and couldn't tell her! That's why Hugo isn't coming back to school!

But . . . why can't Hugo come to school just because his father . . . After all, it isn't Hugo's fault.

What can Hugo's daddy have done?

Karin certainly knows. After all, her daddy is a policeman. It must have been he, of course, who put Hugo's daddy away. Oh, it's horrible even to think about it.

That was why Karin wasn't allowed to say anything.

Now Josephine understands Karin. She couldn't have told, either. A good thing it wasn't Papa-Father who . . .

Blushing for shame, Josephine remembers how she once tried to make Karin believe that Papa-Father, too, could put people in prison. She thought it sounded impressive then. It was because Karin had said that a clergyman and a policeman were more or less the same thing.

Her thoughts rush about in her head.

Maybe it isn't true? Maybe it's all just a nasty lie, made up to . . . to . . .

No, why should May-Lise invent such a thing? Didn't she want to be friends with Josephine? And she said it was as true as could be. For her mother had heard it from the policeman's wife, who works at the post office. That is to say, from Karin's mother.

What has Hugo's father done?

And why must Hugo . . .?

She'll have to try and find out more from May-Lise tomorrow.

Her thoughts go round and round . . .

But the next day May-Lise is with Berit again. Ulla is either by herself or else hangs about listlessly near any little group that happens to collect. She looks unhappy and unfriendly, as usual.

Berit and May-Lise don't even look towards Josephine. For them she's just so much air. As if yesterday had never been. As if May-Lise had never put her arm through Josephine's. As if she had never whispered her secret to her. As if . . .

Yes, it's all beyond belief. Incomprehensible.

Josephine has never felt so lonely.

During lessons she can't take her eyes off May-Lise's pretty little person. But May-Lise doesn't even meet her glance today, doesn't smile as she did yesterday.

Then Josephine sees something she'll never forget.

There, fluttering like a butterfly, goes May-Lise about the playground with Berit at her heels and her eyes wide open, moving from one to another.

With her hands cupped in front of her mouth, she whispers something in ear after ear while Berit looks on.

All through break she is at it, running from one to another.

Once Josephine hears a few words:

'It's a terribly secret secret, of course. You mustn't repeat it to *anyone*.' Then May-Lise cups her little hand and whispers into the eagerly listening ear. Whispers the secret which she could tell only her best friend!

Suddenly Josephine fancies the earth is rocking beneath her feet. She doesn't feel well.

Gunnel comes loping across the playground. Chewing gum, insolent and scornful. Fortunately, she seems to be in a hurry, but she has time to hiss at Josephine:

'Beastly little Anna!'

Josephine is like a lost soul. Break seems endless. She wanders aimlessly about outside the schoolhouse.

Suddenly she stands face to face with Karin.

'Hello,' says Karin, hesitantly.

'Hello,' Josephine replies. Also a bit shyly.

She looks around for Karin's new friend. But Karin, it appears, is alone.

'Josephine,' says Karin, 'I want to be friends again.'

'So do I,' says Josephine.

'It was silly of me,' whispers Karin.

'Of me, too.'

'I was silliest.'

'No, you weren't.'

'Yes, I was, but daddy had told me not to tell anyone. I'd promised him, and I got angry when you wouldn't believe me.'

'Do you always keep your promises?' asks Josephine.

'Yes, of course I do. Don't you?'

'Ye-es.'

They walk silently together a while, wondering. Then Karin asks:

'Josephine, do you know about it now – about Hugo?'

'Yes, now everyone does.'

'It isn't my fault,' says Karin. 'It must be somebody else who's been telling tales.'

Josephine nods:

'It's a good thing it isn't you. And that you didn't tell me, either,' she adds.

Then they fall silent again.

'Are you friends with May-Lise now?' Karin asks, suddenly.

Josephine doesn't answer immediately.

'Are you?' repeats Karin.

'No,' Josephine answers in a hard voice.

'With me, then?'

'Yes.'

# 15

THEY have a day off because the school is being cleaned. Josephine is allowed to go to town with Papa-Father.

He has a lot of things to do, and she's to go to the dentist and the hairdresser's. Outside the church they get on the bus. The morning is grey and cold, but it's cosy inside the bus. It feels lovely to sit beside Papa-Father in the soft seats and look out over the country-side.

Frost lies on the roofs of the houses, on trees, bushes, and fences. The day is so dark they can see lights shining inside the windows of houses, even though it's past ten o'clock in the morning. The lights are on in the bus, too.

When people get on and off, their breath is like smoke. The windows get steamy, and Josephine keeps wiping the window-pane with her glove.

It takes a whole hour to get to town. As far as Josephine is concerned, it could take twice as long, the trip is such fun.

The bus stops in the market place. The dentist doesn't live far away, and Papa-Father accompanies Josephine there. But he doesn't wait for her. He hasn't time. She will have to go to the hairdresser's alone. It's the next house.

When she's finished she'll have to walk by herself the little way back to the market place and meet Papa-Father in the restaurant there. They've just passed it, so Josephine will find her way all right.

It's in the Grand Hotel.

'So we'll meet there and have something nice to eat. You can have cake or ice cream for dessert, if it isn't too cold for ice cream today,' Papa-Father said.

Josephine doesn't think it's too cold. They agree to meet there at half past one, in the restaurant.

'If I'm not there when you come, just go in and sit down at a nice table and wait for me. You can order something to nibble on in the meantime.'

Papa-Father leaves her, and a moment later Josephine finds herself in the dentist's office. She hasn't a single cavity, so she gets a big bookmark with an elephant on it, for taking such good care of her teeth.

Then she goes happily off to the hairdresser's. There she has to wait a while, but it doesn't take long to get her hair cut. Not much of her hair is *to be* cut, because at home they want her to have long hair.

When Josephine is finished at the hairdresser's it is still only half past twelve. She won't be meeting Papa-Father for almost an hour, but, since she doesn't own a watch, she doesn't know that.

She is already ravenously hungry, so she goes straight to the market place.

GRAND HOTEL is written there in huge letters over a door. That's it! In she goes.

Now she is standing in a big lobby with deep arm-chairs, looking rather lost. She sees no one, except herself in the gigantic mirror on the wall.

Suddenly a man appears behind a long counter at one end of the lobby. He smiles at her.

'What would you like, my little friend?' He asks.

'I'm to have dinner here with my father,' Josephine answers.

'Then I'll show you the way to the dining room,' says the friendly gentleman, and walks in front of Josephine to a couple of doors, which open silently. Then they enter a dining room that is as big as an ocean and ever so lovely. All the tables are decked with white tablecloths and flowers in tall vases. From the ceiling hang gleaming crystal chandeliers, and at the far end of the room a man is playing a big grand piano. It is all very grand and solemn.

'Can you see your father?' asks the man.

Not many people are in here. A couple close to the wall. And a solitary fat man reading the newspaper. Josephine realizes that the friendly man thinks this fatty is her father.

'My father is thin,' she informs him. 'He isn't here yet, but he said I should wait for him here.'

'That's quite all right,' says the man, choosing a nice table with yellow carnations and a little lamp on it, not far from the piano.

'Will this do?' he asks, holding the chair for Josephine to sit down.

'Yes, thank you,' she says. 'I should have something to nibble, too, my father said.'

'Just a moment,' says the man, and goes up to another man in a white jacket, who at once comes over to Josephine with a menu.

'Here's today's menu, Miss,' he says, bowing.

He's the most handsome man Josephine has ever set eyes on in all her life. He looks like a fairy story prince. His hair, which stands up all round his head, is a mass of fair little curls. He is pink in the face and has pale-blue eyes. And on his white jacket are gold buttons.

All these colours are so lovely. When he bends down to light the lamp and the glow from the red silk lamp-shade falls on him, he positively seems to shine. Josephine stares, smiling and enchanted.

'I suppose you can read?' he asks.

'Of course I can.' Josephine wakes from her trance and begins sounding out the words on the menu, in a loud voice:

'Grand Hotel Bro-kop-ing. Lunch – bread, butter, three hors, hors … hors d'oeuv-res – entree – eight comma zero zero kro-nor, butt-er cheese, her-ring plate, en-tree eight-five-zero kron-or ...'

In a friendly voice the fairy-story prince interrupts her:

'Well, I see you can read,' he says, praising her efforts. 'Now, I wonder, would you like to have bread and butter or little sandwiches?'

'I'd like some of those you don't have to spread the food on yourself. And my father said I could have ice-cream too.'

'But that would be for dessert, wouldn't it?'

Josephine nods. Then he asks her what she wants to drink, milk or lemonade. She chooses lemonade.

He leaves her, but soon he is back again with three tiny doll's sandwiches and her lemonade.

It doesn't take her more than a minute to get these inside her – leaving her just as hungry as she was before. Immediately, he comes over with the menu again, and she reads:

'Om ... om-elette with spin-ach, fried plaice with parsley and but-ter, calf's liv-er à la ... That à la is everywhere,' she says. She has never had that.

'What is à la?' she asks. 'It sounds good, I think I'll have some of that.'

'Not spinach omelette or plaice, then?'

'Yes, I'll take that too,' says Josephine as an after-thought.

'Which?'

'Both of course,' says Josephine. 'They're both on the list, aren't they?'

One after the other Josephine gobbles up a lovely yellow omelette and a marvellous fish. Then comes the à la, and tastes like liver. She eats half of each of her portions, leaving the other half for Papa-Father. Why isn't he here, anyway?

The fairy-story prince takes away the empty lemonade bottle and brings a new one. He's wonderful. Everything here is wonderful.

It's he who gives orders around here. He moves tables and plates about and changes tablecloths just as he likes.

Josephine takes a look at the other guests. Fatty has gone. But a pretty lady has come instead. An incredibly pretty lady. There she sits with a wretched little glass in front of her, looking miserable. Why didn't she get a big glass, like the one he gave Josephine? It's not fair. Josephine is sorry for her.

But then, she hasn't got the fairy-story prince, either. A perfectly ordinary pale man with flat hair is serving her. A meany, of course. He doesn't even let her have a big glass. How sorry Josephine feels for her! She'll tell the prince about him, and he can deal with the mean old fellow over there. She gives him a treacherous look.

Then she starts spelling out the menu again.

It says you can have pancakes as well. Her favourites!

At once she orders some from the fairy-story prince.

'Aren't you going to finish up all these other courses first? You've a lot left.'

Then Josephine explains: that's for Papa-Father when he arrives.

'Oh, I see,' says the prince, thoughtfully. 'I'll have a word with the head-waiter.'

*The head-waiter!* Who's he? So her prince has a head-waiter working for him!

Again she looks at the poor lady. No one has brought her anything, only the little glass that is almost empty. Not even a bottle on her table. And Josephine has had two whole bottles of lemonade! Perhaps she should go over and offer the lady some? The poor thing looks more and more miserable. She stares in despair at the man who is playing the piano. Unfortunately Josephine can't see what he looks like, as his back is turned to her. But the lady can see him, and to judge from her unhappy expression he can't be much to look at. Though he does play rather well. The lady, poor thing, just smokes and smokes. She has to have something to do since everyone is so mean to her.

But Josephine is radiant. Here comes the prince with her pancakes. And strawberry jam. Just the same, she doesn't forget the lady. In a whisper she implores the prince to give the lady some pancakes, too, and a big glass instead.

'I'm afraid it isn't my table,' he says, with a smile.

'But ... aren't all the tables yours?' asks Josephine, surprised.

'I don't have time for them all, you see. It would be too much for me,' he says.

Of course. After all he *is* a prince, and can't be expected to attend to everyone. But it must be very sad for the poor lady.

What lovely pancakes! She eats them all up – there must certainly be more somewhere for Papa-Father. She would have liked some more herself. Eating in restaurants makes you hungry. She takes another look at the menu. Just in case there's anything she hasn't eaten. And so there is. Almost too much food. There's cold braised ham and à la, though of course she's had that, and lobster and beef à la again. And trout.

Then comes duckling. That sounds delicious. But it would be too much, if she has to have all the rest too. She must ask the prince if she can skip those courses. She hopes his feelings won't be hurt.

No, he's decent about it. She can skip the rest by all means. So she orders the duckling.

'Wouldn't it be better if you waited until your father comes?' he asks.

'My father said I should have something to nibble on while I was waiting. And now I've finished everything.' Josephine explains.

So he brings her some duckling. It is just as tasty as the pancakes, with the same lovely jam, too. She orders another bottle of lemonade. She is thirsty, eating so much. Now the duckling is gone, too, as well as all the jam.

At last she begins to feel she has had enough. Almost more than enough.

She sips at her big glass and looks over at the lady. After a while Josephine, too, begins to feel a little sad.

She can hardly get the lemonade down. Maybe it's the same for the lady? Maybe she's eaten too much, too. The thought hadn't occurred to Josephine before. Perhaps that's why she can't manage more than a little glass? Next time the fairy-story prince comes over, Josephine says:

'May I have one of those little doll's glasses, please, like the lady over there has?'

And she gets one.

When, at long last, Papa-Father comes in, he sees Josephine sitting there with a melancholy look on her face and a little wineglass in her hand.

'I thought you'd never come! I've waited and waited,' she complains.

'And I thought I'd never find you. I've looked and looked,' he replies.

'But you said we were to meet at the hotel.'

'Yes, at the snack bar. This is the dining room. The snack bar is next door.'

'But you said the *Grand* Hotel.'

'The snack bar is part of the hotel, too. But it doesn't matter. The main thing is that we've found each other. Poor Josephine, have you had anything to eat?'

Delighted, Josephine shows him the menu.

'They let me skip the lobster and the trout,' she explains. 'It didn't matter. They weren't upset.'

Astounded, Papa-Father stares at the menu, and from the menu to the plates with half an omelette, half the plaice, some liver, and some duckling still waiting on the table.

'I've saved all this for you,' Josephine explains generously. 'And I haven't had my ice cream yet. I've saved it till you came.'

Papa-Father bursts out laughing.

'You're really the last word, Josephine,' he says, wiping the tears from his eyes. 'You'll be the ruin of your old father, but what does it matter? Are you sure you have room for the ice cream?'

Yes, she is quite sure. And Papa-Father talks to the fairy-tale prince and the head-waiter, who also comes over. He says:

'Now my greedy little daughter wants some ice cream. Can she have some?'

Josephine turns bright red in the face and gives Papa-

Father a gentle kick under the table. What will they think of her?

But they just smile, and the Prince says it has been 'a real pleasure' to serve Josephine. Which makes her blush with pride.

Then Papa-Father gets some fresh hot food, and Josephine her ice cream. And they have a lovely time together. Talking about everything.

Papa-Father has a funny name for the prince – 'a

waiter' he calls him. But not so loud that he can hear.

And just imagine – he doesn't think the lady is pretty at all! Nor does he think she's unhappy, either. It's just her make-up, he says.

In the end Papa-Father thanks Josephine for coming to the wrong place.

'It's much more fun here than in the snack bar,' he says.

And they leave. The head-waiter and the prince stand bowing to them. And the prince holds the swinging door open for them. In the hall the friendly man helps them on with their coats. Everyone smiles and says they're looking forward to seeing them there again.

Soon they are sitting in the bus.

It is dark outside, now. Pitch black. All along the way lights wink at them secretly from the little windows of houses.

And in the sky thousands of stars are twinkling down, too.

# 16

Now the whole school knows that Hugo's father has gone to prison. All day long they do nothing but whisper about it. Some even speak of it quite openly. Gunnel, for instance.

'I knew it, I knew it in my bones,' she says, delighted that someone else is in trouble.

'How could you?' asks one of her henchmen.

'Oh, it wasn't so hard to tell that there was something wrong with the kid.'

Feeling herself safer in the saddle, Gunnel becomes utterly insufferable.

'Obviously, he can't come back to school,' she says. 'After all, who would want to have anything to do with him? Except Silly Anna, of course.'

'My mother would never let me,' squeaks Berit, proper and respectable as ever.

'Nor mine either,' says May-Lise.

All the others in the group agree. No, no one would be allowed to speak to him. Not on your life!

It is early morning, before the first lesson. It has been raining all night; the sky is overcast and the ground misty. It is still not quite light. Suddenly, Josephine comes in through the school gates; and Gunnel's eyes narrow to slits:

'SILLY ANNA'S LOST HER SPANNER!' She yells.

All the others burst out into a shriek of laughter, yelling at the top of their voices:

'SILLY ANNA, SILLY ANNA, SILLY ANNA LOST HER SPANNER!'

None of this is particularly witty or insulting, but it has a paralysing effect on Josephine. She doesn't know where to turn. All at once she feels utterly defenceless. She stands there, looking lamely about her, quite lost. But this only encourages the others to go on. Even the ones who are usually decent get excited at the smell of blood.

'It's a *grey* day today, chaps!' squawks a usually quiet little boy, making a play on Anna's name. Because Grå in Swedish means 'Gray'.

'Grey-day! Grey-day!'

'It's getting greyer every day,' says another wag.

'It's not surprising, when we've got a Gray at school.'

Gunnel stands there silently, her eyes darting hither

and thither. Now and again the others look towards her to catch her approving glances. From Gunnel emanates a strange power that excites even the most good-natured of them.

As for Gunnel herself, she just waits for the right moment to intervene. It will be she who will give the death-blow. All else is just a preparation.

'Yes, and she has *grey* gloves on, too,' titters pretty little May-Lise.

'Quite right,' says Gunnel slowly, emphasizing every word. And with narrowing eyes approaches Josephine.

Josephine is terrified out of her wits and tries to run, but all she can manage is a halting little trot.

Like a hawk, Gunnel is upon her.

'Silly Anna! Isn't it enough being called Grå? Do you have to wear grey gloves too? Give them here!'

The murmurs from the others grow quieter. Now comes the exciting part.

'Give them here, I say!'

Josephine puts up as much resistance as she can, but in the end Gunnel pulls off her gloves. Triumphantly she holds them up for inspection. Everyone cheers. Then she throws the gloves in a puddle and stamps on them.

How dare she? The others, tense, but slightly scared, take a step back. What will she do now?

Holding the dripping wet gloves, Gunnel goes up to

Josephine, who desperately tries to retrieve them.

'You'll get them back all right!' snaps Gunnel. 'Here, take a whiff of these!' she cries, and hits Josephine on the face and hands with the soaking gloves. Josephine stands rooted to the spot. She hardly grasps what is happening to her.

Suddenly, between the wet slaps, a voice is heard. Someone tugs violently at Gunnel, so that she loses her balance and falls backward into the puddle of water.

'What are you doing to Josephine, you bully!'

There stands Hugo, big as life. In his big black rain cape, bits of string and all. Just as he always is. His cowlick sticking up. His eyes unusually blue.

But now the words come pouring out of him as he shouts her down. And Gunnel just sits in her rain puddle as if struck by lightning.

'And that's the best place for you, you miserable scarecrow. Hitting someone who's so much smaller than you! There must be something wrong inside your head. Are you crazy?'

All around Hugo a dead silence reigns. All the faces, formerly so triumphant, now look unsure of themselves, sheepish.

Gunnel gradually recovers herself and clambers out of the puddle. Her behind is rather wet, but she's determined not to give in without a struggle.

Now she tries to look scornful, but her eyes won't

narrow in quite the properly convincing way.

'I despise you,' she says. 'Isn't your father in jail?'
Someone in the cluster of children gasps. Otherwise it's
frighteningly quiet. A little dark cloud passes across
Hugo's face. His eyes are so vividly blue that Gunnel
can't stand their gaze, and looks away.

'Well, isn't he?'

'Yes, he is,' says Hugo, calmly. He raises his voice:
'And do you know why? He's there for fighting. He
punched a fellow who got a bit too sure of himself
and began bothering others. It's easy to punch a little

too hard, that's all. Some people ought to be glad they get off with a wet bottom!'

A laugh is heard. Then another. And another.

In the end the whole cluster of children is laughing. The laughter spreads all over the school playground. Laughter of relief.

Jubilant, everyone gathers round Hugo. Then they all march in triumph upstairs to their classroom. Hugo goes back to his desk beside Josephine.

Teacher is one huge radiant smile.

'Welcome back, Hugo,' she says. 'We've all missed you terribly.'

'Have you?' answers Hugo, looking totally unconcerned, even if he isn't.

Then teacher sends Edvin Pettersson off to buy sweets and gingerbread biscuits. They can all eat as much as they like, while teacher reads them a story.

The whole day turns into a tremendous celebration.

# 17

JOSEPHINE has told Karin about her visit to the restaurant. At home she has told Mama and Mandy, too. But it's more fun telling Karin, who listens to it all with proper seriousness and understands what a superior sort of pleasure it was. A lofty and distinguished pleasure. This is something Mama and Mandy don't understand; when they hear about it they just laugh.

But Karin is enormously impressed, wants to know all about the carpets and the crystal chandeliers and the mirrors.

'It was a palace,' she says. 'And the beautiful lady must have been a film star.' Yes, of course that's what she was, though it hadn't occurred to Josephine.

Together they contemplate the menu, which the prince had given Josephine to take home. They read it over again and again.

'And did they really let you eat everything?' Karin asks enviously.

'Yes. And the best part of it all was, you didn't have to eat what you didn't like. They didn't nag at all. You just left it out.'

'I don't believe it.'

'Well, that's how it was. They were ever so nice. I had pancakes with jam *and* duckling. And ice cream afterwards.'

Karin looks dreamy.

'It must have been like Mr Svensson the shopkeeper's fiftieth birthday party, though of course I wasn't invited. But my father and mother were there, and they talked about it for months afterwards.'

Suddenly Karin gives Josephine a melancholy look.

'They'd never let me eat that much,' she says. 'My mother always says I must think of my figure. Doesn't yours say that?'

'No.'

'How happy you must be,' sighs Karin. 'Though of course you may not get married. For my mother says all girls have to think of their figures, otherwise they won't get married. They call it dieting. Even my mother does it, though she's married already.'

Josephine pricks up her ears. All this is news to her. Why hasn't anyone told her about such important matters? She definitely wants to get married.

'What do you do when you diet?' she asks, seriously.

'You aren't allowed to eat very much and you must

131

never stop thinking about your figure.'

But that's . . . that's dreadful! Josephine *never* thinks about her figure! Think how she ate in that restaurant!

In her imagination she suddenly sees the fat man who was sitting there at his table. Perhaps that's how you get fat, eating in a restaurant.

'Am I fat, Karin?' she asks anxiously.

Karin examines Josephine, puts her arms around Josephine's waist and, with a deeply serious expression on her face, feels her friend's tummy. Her examination

continues with extreme thoroughness, while Josephine looks more and more worried.

'Am I?' she insists.

'A little, maybe . . .'

'And that means I won't ever be married?'

'Well, you'd better begin to diet right away,' Karin says consolingly, 'then you'll still have a chance. It's much easier if there's two of you doing it, my mother says. She wants the whole family to, but Papa doesn't want to.'

Josephine weighs her chances of getting everyone at the vicarage to start dieting, but finds them rather slim. After all, Mandy is the only one who's fat, and that's how she *should* be. Otherwise she wouldn't be Mandy.

Papa-Father and Mama aren't fat. Not a bit. And they wouldn't start dieting just for her sake. No. She'd better start dieting together with Karin right away.

'It's a good thing you told me,' she says, then. 'But what do we do? I don't know anything about it.'

'First you have to plan a diet. That's most important of all,' says Karin, full of energy. She tears out a page from her exercise book, sits down, and chews thoughtfully on her pen.

'They have to be *strict* rules,' she says. Josephine gives a serious nod.

'Do you think they ought to be secret?'

Yes, Karin is quite sure they should. Otherwise all

the others will start copying them and begin to diet too. Berit and May-Lise, for example. And that would be frightful.

'Are you going to write, or shall I?' Karin asks.

'You. You've got nicer handwriting.'

'Have I?' says Karin, flattered, and putting the tip of her tongue in one cheek, begins to write. They invent the rules together. Each point is seriously discussed, until at last they agree on the following diet:

DYET FoR JoSEPHINE aND KARIN

1. 9 SANNWITCHES A DAY Not 10.

2. ONLI THREE HELPINGS AT DINER.

3. DYET fOr WON MUNTH.

4. AT MIDSUMMR WE CAN haVe 5 HELPINGS aT DINER

5. *No* PORRIG IN THE MORNING WhEN WE EAT iN THE KITCHEN AND NOBODDY SEeS US THEN WE CAN HAV SOME SANNWICHES INSTED.

6. FORE POtATOS WEN WE HAVE POTATOS.

7. AT CRISMUS WE CAN HAVE LOTS OF PORRIG IF WEV ROOM BUT NO GOOS STUFFING IT TASTS AwFUL ANd ISNT GOOD FOR DYeTING

8. NOT TOO MUCH CREEM OR SHUGGER ANd THINGS THAT MAK YOU FAT.

9. WE musnt EAT MUCH IN THE EVENING ONLY SANNWITCHES AND milk.

10. WE BEGIN ARE DYET TMORROW NOV-eMBR 21est THAT MEANS WENSDAY.

11. GO For A WALK AT LEAST ONCE A MUNTH aND SHOULD BE ONCE A WEAK.

12. DO FIZZICLE EXERSIZES TOO

13. NEVER FORGET TOO DYeT!!

With great pride, they read over their list several times. Josephine is allowed to take it home with her, to copy.

All evening long she sits slaving away, trying to make her writing as nice as Karin's. When she's finished she stuffs the rules away in the bottom of her drawer, among her other treasures. There she notices the menu.

For a while she stands there, deep in thought, with the menu in one hand and her diet list in the other. Then she seizes her pencil and adds one more rule. One that is deadly secret, which even Karin mustn't know about. Just for safety's sake:

14. IF I GO TO THE RESTRONT I ONLI NEED TO DYET A LITTLE BIT I MUSSnT HAVE A LA OR FISH AND CAN EAT SevRL HELPINGS oF PANCAK AnD DUCK-LING INSTEAD BECUZ THEY DOnT MAK YOU FaT.

# *18*

It's dark in the mornings now, as it is in Sweden in midwinter. But Hugo comes to the vicarage every morning and has something to eat with Mandy and Josephine before he and Josephine go off to school. Papa-Father has arranged for this, so that Josephine shan't have to walk alone in the dark. It is also because Hugo has such a long way to walk through the forest that, by the time he has reached the vicarage, he is really hungry.

Sometimes he comes back with Josephine after school, too, and has some hot chocolate to drink before he goes on home.

Everyone at the vicarage likes Hugo – especially Mandy. When he gets there in the morning, his cheeks glow after his long walk through the woods. His hair stands up on end, and his clothes, which are much too big for him, bring in a fresh scent of pinewoods and wind.

Hugo is an early bird. So is Mandy, and usually only Mandy is up and about when Hugo arrives. Then he helps her bring in firewood and light the fire and mend things that have been broken. Often he brings Mandy a present, which he has carved himself.

His friends at the vicarage are beginning to understand that Hugo is no ordinary schoolboy. He is a natural spirit, who by some happy chance has turned up at school.

One morning it's pitch dark outside. Hugo arrives with a stable lantern to light their way to school.

Everything is remarkably quiet. On either side of the road the forest is black as night. The sky, too, is dark. Hugo swings his lantern into the darkness so that the damp trunks of trees glisten and gleam, and a secret light flashes and blinks in ditches and puddles.

He tells Josephine all about the mysterious creatures that hide in the woods. But in his company there's no need for her to be frightened. The men in his family have all been charcoal burners working in the woods. He is a friend of all the forest dwellers.

Josephine feels quite safe, even though she fancied she saw the Wood Spirit's hair fluttering among the tree trunks. Or was it the gleam of Hugo's lantern?

Suddenly Hugo says:

'I had a letter from my father. They have new cur-

tains in the prison now. Red and blue striped ones.
Very pretty, he says.'

Josephine is so surprised that she doesn't answer.
Hugo is talking about the prison as if nothing in the

world were more natural than to be inside it. It makes
her feel embarrassed.

But Hugo goes on talking about his father.

'He'll be coming home at Christmas, so it won't be
long now. Then he won't try any more town-life, that's

for sure. Charcoal burners don't like working in a factory, you see.'

Once again he makes a sweep with his lantern towards the darkness of the woods.

'The forest is something you've got to stick with,' he says. 'If you don't, things'll turn out bad. But it wasn't his fault, really it wasn't, it was an accident, you see. It could happen to the best of us. That's what your dad says, too.'

Papa-Father! Josephine is completely astounded. Has he had something to do with all this?

Yes, he has. Everything. Hugo tells her that on the day when Josephine and her father were in town, he went to see Hugo's father in prison. And afterwards he went to a coffee shop with Hugo and his mother.

So Hugo was in town that day too! And Josephine knew nothing about it! Papa-Father hadn't said a word. So this was what he had been doing while Josephine was at the dentist's and the hairdresser's. And that's why she had to wait so long in the restaurant, too.

And this must mean that Papa-Father knew Hugo, too, though he had never said a word about it. But, as a matter of fact, Josephine hadn't said so much about Hugo at home, either. To begin with, they had come late to school so often that she had thought it best to hold her tongue about knowing him. And then, when she heard about his father being in jail, she felt still less like talking. She thought they might not have liked it. How silly of her! And how little she knew Papa-Father!

Now she is immensely relieved and has to smile at the thought that she and Papa-Father had been keeping the same secret from each other, all this time.

Hugo, too, is very happy today. He walks along, imagining what a lovely time they'll have together when his father comes home at Christmas.

He holds up the lantern, so that Josephine can see how nice it is. It belonged to both his father and his grandfather. But now it is Hugo's.

'My father wrote that in this letter, see. Now I can have it to find my way to school,' he says proudly.

# 19

It's already the ninth of December. And the name in the calendar for that day is 'Anna'. But Josephine doesn't know this, for the simple reason that they never celebrated the day at home. After all, she doesn't want to be called Anna; so they celebrate her 'name-day' on August the twenty-first, instead, because the name for that day is 'Josephina'.

So off she goes to school, suspecting nothing.

When the blue doors are thrown open and they all march into the classroom, she sees something that makes her turn pale and then scarlet.

Right in the middle of the blackboard the teacher has drawn a pretty, flowery garland, and in the centre is written, in big red letters, that dreadful name: ANNA.

There's nothing unusual about this. Teacher does it every time anyone has a birthday or name day, but it never occurred to Josephine that some day she would do it for 'Anna'.

Now she knows what's in store for her. And it makes her tremble in every limb.

The First Sunday in Advent is already past, and the little Advent candles are standing on their desks. For a candlestick Josephine has a little old china goblin, which she loves very much for it was Mama's when she was little.

Now the teacher asks them to light their candles, and she herself lights just one of the four candles on a miniature Christmas tree standing on the harmonium. This is what people do in Sweden during the first week in Advent.

Then she sits down to play. They have to sing *Prepare a Way for the Lord*, the loveliest tune Josephine knows. They usually sing it with Papa-Father in church.

But now she stands there petrified, frightened of that horrible word on the blackboard, frightened of the faces her classmates will make at her.

The hymn is over. Teacher gets up and says the Lord's Prayer. Then she says the Blessing.

Josephine stands, head bowed, very reverently. Much more reverently than usual. Usually she is paying attention to what the teacher is saying. But today she doesn't have the remotest idea of what the teacher's saying. Everything just goes round and round and gets hotter and hotter inside her head, and she wishes the prayer would never come to an end, would last for ever. But it doesn't.

Now it's over. A scraping of feet, a banging of desk-tops. Then Miss Sund claps her hands. She says:

'Everybody stand up!'

More scraping. Those who have already sat down get up again.

Josephine stands with her head bowed and arms hanging down.

The teacher goes on:

'Before we begin our work, we must cheer for some-one who's name day it is today.'

Josephine feels everyone's eyes upon her. They are sticking into her back like needles. Into her arms. Legs. Eyelids. Throat. Cheeks. Everywhere. This is the worst thing she has ever been through at school!

The teacher's eyes hurt worst of all. They make her forehead and whole head burn. Not for anything in the world could she look up and meet them, as she should.

Now Miss Sund says in her friendly voice:

'Anna Grå! Three cheers for Anna who has her name day today. Hip hip . . .'

'HURRAH! HURRAH! HURRAH!' and a couple of little belated hurrahs afterwards, from the class.

Then silence. Everyone waits. They are waiting for

her to turn to the class and curtsy and smile and thank them for their kindness.

But Josephine just stands there.

'Well, Anna dear? What do you say?' asks the teacher, kindly.

Then Josephine gets furious. Why should she have to put up with this? Just because the teacher has thought it up? Why does everyone have to celebrate each other's birthdays and name days? Aren't these a private affair?

She looks up, her eyes darkening; peers defiantly around at the class, and finally meets teacher's eye.

'My name isn't Anna,' she says harshly.

The teacher looks at her with astonishment.

'Oh yes it is,' she says.

'No,' says Josephine firmly.

The whole class begins to buzz with disapproval. But out of the murmurs Hugo's voice gradually makes itself heard.

'No, her name isn't Anna. Her name's Josephine. What's the matter? Didn't you hear her?'

'That's just what she *calls* herself,' says a superior little voice. It's Berit.

'What's the difference between having a name and being called something?' Hugo asks.

'Obviously,' says Berit, who is the tidiest little girl in

the class, 'if you're christened something, that's what your name is. And she wasn't christened Josephine. She was christened Anna.'

Then Hugo laughs.

'That's news to me! If it was just a matter of being christened, then I wouldn't have any name at all. But I dare anyone to say my name isn't Hugo.'

As he enunciates his own name, Hugo looks round, proud and ready to fight all comers.

Silence. A candle sputters. Not another sound for a whole minute.

Josephine holds her head high as she stands there. And she smiles. Suddenly the teacher smiles too. With a sudden motion she turns to the blackboard and wipes out the name Anna in its flowery garland. Seizing her red chalk, she writes in clear elegant letters: JOSE-PHINE.

A new murmur is heard from the class, not a disapproving one now. Only Berit's voice tries to put up some resistance, though it doesn't sound too sure of itself.

'Yes, but her name isn't really Josephine. It's . . .'

Then the teacher interrupts:

'I think Hugo is quite right,' she says thoughtfully. 'Actually, it doesn't make much difference what one's name is. Whether our name is nice or not depends on ourselves, doesn't it?'

But Hugo waves his hand in protest.

He says in a loud voice:

'There isn't much truth in those words, Miss. That's just a lot of talk made up by grown-ups to make us kids behave ourselves.'

'Well, and shouldn't children behave themselves?' asks Miss Sund.

'Maybe so. Maybe not. But there's no point trying to trick them into it. If I wasn't allowed to be called Hugo, I'd be a pack of trouble, I'll have you know.'

And that, as far as Hugo is concerned, is the end of the matter. He sits down and takes out his books. The others, not knowing what to do, scrape their feet. The candles flutter. The teacher clears her throat. She looks at Josephine and asks Hugo to get up again. She tells the class to be silent, and says:

'Before we begin our work today, I think we ought to cheer Josephine. It's not her name day, but since that falls in the summer holidays, perhaps we should take the opportunity and do it today. *Three cheers for Josephine*. Hip hip . . .'

'HURRAH! HURRAH! HURRAH!' and a tremendous series of hurrahs follows from the whole class.

Josephine curtsies and smiles and thanks them, as she should. She doesn't find it at all difficult now.

From that day on everyone calls her Josephine. It has been a long, hard struggle, but Josephine – that is, Hugo and Josephine – has won in the end.

## 20

THERE is to be a Christmas party at school, so Hugo and Josephine are in a hurry.

Songs have been practised every day. And Hugo has cut down a big fir tree, which he and Josephine have dragged to school. Then they had to make sweets and candy to hang on the tree. The teacher showed them how to do it.

They were so busy with the party that they hadn't time for anything else before the Christmas holidays.

And then there is the day of Lucia, who comes to Sweden in the midwinter darkness with a crown of burning candles on her head, on December the thirteenth.

'We must choose our Lucia,' says teacher one day. She is red in the face and her hair stands up on end. She's just as excited about all this as the children are, and she doesn't get the least bit irritated, even though children are running about and jostling her all the time. Everyone is asking for things, asking for help at the same time.

Josephine wonders how she could have ever made so silly a mistake as to wonder whether Miss Sund was a real teacher. Now she can't imagine her as anything else.

Teacher looks around the class.

'Yes,' she says again, 'it's time we chose our Lucia.' And her eyes come to rest on Josephine.

'I suggest we choose Josephine, because she has such long fair hair. Or have you other suggestions?'

Josephine blushes violently and doesn't dare look at the others. She can't believe it's true.

Teacher chooses her.

For a moment, silence falls on the class. Then various comments are heard. Josephine sits with her heart in her throat. She hears protests, which grow louder and louder. The names of other girls fly about in the air.

'Ann-Mari,' someone suggests.

'May-Lise.'

'No, Ruth,' says another.

'Berit! Kerstin! Marianne!'

They can't agree. But no one utters Josephine's name. Hugo says he thinks teacher should decide, but it's no use. There's a tremendous uproar in the class. There always is, when Lucia has to be chosen.

Teacher knocks on her desk.

'Be quiet! Silence in the class!' she calls out. 'I've said what I think, but if we can't all agree, then we'll have to have a vote.'

Then she hands out little pieces of paper for everyone to write down the name of the girl they want to have as Lucia.

Josephine's heart thuds. Her cheeks are burning, but as the teacher walks past her desk she feels a little pat on her head. Josephine meets her teacher's happy glance, and her cheeks cease burning.

There's no point in wondering who they're going to pick. May-Lise of course. May-Lise is fickle. But she *is* the prettiest girl in the class. And has curly hair. And big eyes.

When they have written down the names, they fold the little slips of paper, and the teacher collects them in a hat. It looks funny, because it's a blue hat with a bouncing pom-pom. Ulla's hat.

Then the teacher sits down at her desk and pours out all the slips in front of her. She unfolds them and sorts them out into heaps. One heap for each name.

It's all terribly exciting. Teacher doesn't say a word about how it's going. Which heap is getting the most votes?

Josephine is keeping her fingers crossed for May-Lise, while the teacher begins counting.

The excitement increases. Miss Sund is ready. She looks out over the class.

It was May-Lise. She won by a single vote over Ruth, who came second. Josephine claps her hands and cheers. One vote – that must have been hers.

But some are dissatisfied with the results, Hugo for example. He doesn't look very pleased. Again and again he thumps his desk with his fist and says:

'That is all wrong!'

At break, Josephine hears that both Hugo Andersson and Edvin Pettersson voted for her. With the teacher's vote, that makes three. It wasn't enough for her to win, but to Josephine these three votes were worth more than all the others put together.

The night before the Christmas party Josephine gets out of bed again and again, just to make sure that everything she has to take with her has been put into her satchel.

There's the white nightie. And the two candles. Josephine is to be one of Lucia's maids of honour, and they always wear white and carry candles. There's the package with her contribution to the Christmas tree. Beautifully sealed with red sealing wax. But she squeezes it anxiously. Supposing she has put the wrong thing inside! And here it is, all sealed!

She'd better open it and have a look.

It's all right. There lies the pretty little china pig. She holds it in her hand a while.

'Who's going to get you tomorrow?' she whispers and wraps it up again in some fresh paper. She lights a candle and drops great lumps of sealing wax all round the package. What fun it is! Soon it'll be time for her to go in to Papa-Father and help him seal the family's presents. And no one else is allowed to come in. Then it will really be Christmas. Josephine sits staring out into the air with a dreamy look on her face. What wonderful times are ahead!

Finally she puts the package back into her satchel, and checks for the last time to see that everything is there. She opens the huge bag of biscuits Mandy has baked. Sniffs at it. Marvellous. It's her contribution to the party. Then she blows out the light and pulls up the blind.

Oh, look! It's snowing outside. Silently she opens the window and takes a little of the snow on the window sill, makes it into a snowball, and throws it out into the garden. At last she shuts the window and creeps back into bed.

A fresh scent of newly fallen snow floats through the room, blending with the odour of sealing wax. Josephine breathes deeply. These lovely scents follow her far into her dreams.

Dressed in his best suit, solemn and polite, Hugo comes and fetches Josephine in the morning. His mother has made him a new coat and trousers out of clothes that used to be his father's. He tells her this, not without pride.

His father has come home now. He arrived yesterday, and brought them such a lot of things for Christmas. They'll have a wonderful Christmas, he says.

By the time they get to school, the teacher has already decorated the Christmas tree and put a marzipan pig in each little paper basket. A pink little pig's face sticks up out of each basket. This rouses a cheer.

Now they change into their costumes. The girls put on their Lucia nighties, because they are all to be maids of honour. And the boys are going to be either star-boys, with long pointed caps on their heads, or else a Christmas elf, called a *tomte*.

Hugo has fought to the last to be a tomte. But the teacher stood firm. He's to be a star-boy. Both he and Edvin Pettersson. Again and again they try to take off their pointed caps, but the teacher keeps her eye on them.

'You and Edvin Pettersson are ideal as star-boys,' she says, slyly, pressing their caps down over their ears.

A long table has been set out in the gym, and they put all their contributions to the party on it. Apples and gingerbread biscuits and buns – everything you can think of. But they're not to eat yet.

First they must walk in the Lucia procession. May-Lise makes a beautiful Lucia. With the crown of burning candles on her head, she goes first. Then come the maids of honour and the star-boys. Then the *tomten*. The children in procession walk along singing, with lighted candles in their hands, all around the school. From classroom to classroom, for today only their class is holding its Christmas party.

When the procession is over, the party begins in earnest. Off come all the pointed caps. So do the *tomte* hoods. Only Lucia wants to keep her crown, but teacher won't let her. It might get broken, because things are getting lively now. They dance round the Christmas tree and play games. And they pass around the Christmas presents. Josephine gets a pretty thimble with flowers on it.

Josephine's pig goes to May-Lise. She is very pleased with it, and Josephine doesn't say a word about having been the one who bought it. That's a secret.

At last the time comes for them to gather around the table in the gym. The lights on the Christmas tree are lit, and there are candles on the table. What a lot of delicious things to eat!

When they have all sampled everything and are feeling rather full, Hugo suddenly steps up from behind the tree. In his hand he has a little glass bowl, which gleams in the light from all the candles. The glass bowl is full of grapes, which gleam like pure gold.

This is Hugo's contribution. Now he approaches, carefully holding the bowl in his hands.

'Father had this with him when he came from town yesterday,' he says, going from one to another and offering them grapes. He has taken the grapes off their stalks already, so they lie in a shiny pyramid.

Everyone feels that these are no ordinary grapes.

There is something inexplicable about them. It is not only the mysterious light from the candles, it is also Hugo's astonishing personality that gives the grapes their strange lustre; everyone feels rather solemn.

Without a word, they each take a grape and eat it thoughtfully. When Hugo comes to the teacher, he bows deeply. Everyone looks at the teacher as she lifts her hand to take one of those marvellous grapes. Everyone wishes he or she could be the one to offer them to her.

'You can take two, Miss,' says Hugo.

Then a great cheer breaks loose. Everyone claps his hands and gives a cheer for Miss Sund, because she really is worthy of getting two. And for Hugo, who understands this.

'Thank you, Hugo dear,' says teacher slowly; and Hugo, apparently unmoved, continues on his round with the bowl.

Last of all he comes to Josephine.

There's only one grape left. But it's the biggest of all, and how it shines!

Hugo scratches his neck and stares at it with a worried look.

'That's odd. I must have made a mistake. There should have been two left. This one's for you.'

He holds out the bowl to Josephine.

'No, you have it,' she says.

'We can share it.'

And Hugo takes his old carving knife out of his pocket and smartly slices the grape in two. Two halves, exactly equal – one for Hugo, one for Josephine.

'That wasn't easy,' he says with a grin.

*Maria Gripe*

If you've enjoyed reading about Hugo and Josephine, make sure you don't miss the other two books in Maria Gripe's trilogy:

**JOSEPHINE** (illus)                                    25p

Here we meet Josephine for the first time, before she's even heard of Hugo, and life isn't very easy for her – in fact sometimes she feels as neglected as the cast-off clothes she wears. One sunny morning, she decides to run away, taking with her a bag of necessities and a very shabby stuffed monkey. With an imagination as lively as Josephine's, everyday happenings turn into quite surprising adventures . . .

**HUGO** (illus)                                          25p

In this last book of the trilogy, Hugo is faced with the problem of what to do about his schooling; he has no mother, and his father is away, and there's so much to do at his wood-land home. He also has to earn his living – but how? The first suggestion comes from his best friend, Josephine.

It's the difference between lucky days and ordinary days that makes life so interesting – and with Hugo and Josephine, days are anything but ordinary . . .

# Ursula Moray Williams

*Piccolo Fiction*

Charles Kingsley
THE WATER BABIES (abridged)          60p

Illustrated with Mabel Lucie Attwell's enchanting coloured drawings, this beautiful big book retells the famous story of Tom, the little chimney sweep, who escapes the clutches of his cruel master and enters the wonderful world of the Water Babies, to meet all kinds of strange and magical creatures, and to have adventures beyond his wildest imaginings.